W9-ASW-879

"You have helped, you have," Kate stammered

"And complicated your life very much in the process," Grevil said dryly.

She stared at him, a warm tide of color creeping into her cheeks because she knew what he meant. He smiled slightly and cupped her face in his hands.

"Please, I think you'd better go," she said in a cracked, unsteady voice.

"I can't, not like this," he said. "The fact is, you touch something in me, Kate," he added, drawing her into his arms. He bent his head and claimed her lips. When he lifted his head at last, Kate swayed in his arms and could only stare at him with her lips parted.

"Shall we go on?" Grevil drawled softly. Kate trembled against his body, her heart dangerously close to answering.

Lindsay Armstrong married an accountant from New Zealand and settled down—if you can call it that—in Australia. A coast-to-coast camping trip later, they moved to a six-hundred-acre mixed-grain property, which they eventually abandoned to the mice and leeches and blackflies. Then, after a winning career at the track with an untried trotter, purchased "mainly because he had blue eyes," they opted for a more conventional family life with their five children in Brisbane, where Lindsay now writes.

Books by Lindsay Armstrong

HARLEQUIN ROMANCE
2443—SPITFIRE
2497—MY DEAR INNOCENT
2582—PERHAPS LOVE
2653—DON'T CALL IT LOVE
2785—SOME SAY LOVE
2876—THE HEART OF THE MATTER

HARLEQUIN PRESENTS
559—MELT A FROZEN HEART
607—ENTER MY JUNGLE
806—SAVED FROM SIN
871—FINDING OUT
887—LOVE ME NOT
927—AN ELUSIVE MISTRESS
951—SURRENDER MY HEART
983—STANDING ON THE OUTSIDE
1039—THE SHADOW OF MOONLIGHT

Don't miss any of our special offers. Write to us at the following address for information on our newest releases.

Harlequin Reader Service
901 Fuhrmann Blvd., P.O. Box 1397, Buffalo, NY 14240
Canadian address: P.O. Box 603,
Fort Erie, Ont. L2A 5X3

When the Night Grows Cold

Lindsay Armstrong

Harlequin Books

TORONTO • NEW YORK • LONDON
AMSTERDAM • PARIS • SYDNEY • HAMBURG
STOCKHOLM • ATHENS • TOKYO • MILAN

Original hardcover edition published in 1987
by Mills & Boon Limited

ISBN 0-373-02893-8

Harlequin Romance first edition March 1988

Copyright © 1987 by Lindsay Armstrong.
Philippine copyright 1987. Australian copyright 1987.
Cover illustration copyright © 1988 by Will Davies.
All rights reserved. Except for use in any review, the reproduction or utilization
of this work in whole or in part in any form by any electronic, mechanical
or other means, now known or hereafter invented, including xerography,
photocopying and recording, or in any information storage or retrieval system,
is forbidden without the permission of the publisher, Harlequin Enterprises
Limited, 225 Duncan Mill Road, Don Mills, Ontario, Canada M3B 3K9. All the
characters in this book have no existence outside the imagination of the
author and have no relation whatsoever to anyone bearing the same name
or names. They are not even distantly inspired by any individual known
or unknown to the author, and all incidents are pure invention.

The Harlequin trademarks, consisting of the words HARLEQUIN ROMANCE
and the portrayal of a Harlequin, are trademarks of Harlequin Enterprises
Limited; the portrayal of a Harlequin is registered in the United States Patent
and Trademark Office and in the Canada Trade Marks Office.

Printed in U.S.A.

CHAPTER ONE

'OH, HELL!' Kate Wiley said.

'What's wrong, Mum?' Her eight-year-old son Matthew stuck his head enquiringly out of the cabin of their truck.

'The crows have got at the milk again, and the bread!' she answered, surveying the cardboard carton of groceries on the ground beside the gate. Each milk bottle had its foil top pecked through and the cellophane bread wrapper had been ripped and large chunks gouged and dismembered from the loaf.

'We need to fix the mail box,' Matt observed. 'That's why Mr O'Grady leaves the stuff on the ground.'

The mail box was a large, white-painted drum fixed sideways to a post, but at present it hung at a drunken angle. And Mr O'Grady was the district mail contractor who also delivered groceries, news-papers—anything that was deliverable, in fact, the ultimate criterion being whether he could fit it into his battered van.

'It wouldn't hurt Mr O'Grady to bring it up to the house,' Kate said tersely and quite unfairly.

'If he did it for us he'd have to do it for everyone,' Matt replied. 'He'd never get done.'

'And all I need at the moment,' Kate muttered beneath her breath, 'is to be reasoned with as if I was eight and you twenty-eight!'

But she caught herself up with a guilty sigh and said, 'You're right, Matt. Want to hop out and give me a hand?' She rummaged in the back of the truck, repeatedly pushing aside their large, shaggy dog and coming up with a hammer, some nails and a piece of wood.

Some time later they stood back to admire their handiwork and Matt said, 'There! As good as new.'

Kate smiled wryly down at him. 'Mmm. I don't know why I didn't do it days ago.'

'Our sign's slipped. Let's fix it, too,' Matt suggested. 'Can I try?'

Kate regarded the faded sign on the wooden gate that said 'Kunnunurra', and handed him the hammer. And while he worked away happily, she leant back against the truck and gazed around.

It was a landscape of space and huge skies, great ploughed paddocks and distant hillsides dotted with the shadows of high cloud. From the gate to the homestead, the half-mile drive wound up a gentle slope covered with tussocky, silver-grey grass and dotted with 'blackboys'—picturesque Australian shrubs. And at the breast of the rise, just visible from the gate, were the tips of the tall old gums that surrounded the house and stables and machinery shed.

From up there the view was even better—one hundred and eighty degrees of Queensland's Darling Downs, one of the richest agricultural areas of Australia, where the volcanic topsoil was deep and fertile, and where summer was hot but not oppressively humid, as it was in Brisbane roughly ninety miles away down the range on the coast. Where winter was cold and the westerlies sometimes blew mercilessly for days on end and frost laid a silver rime on the land.

It was winter now, but it was a landscape that had once enchanted Kate Wiley, whether it was cloaked in summer green and acres and acres of golden wheat, or rather stark and bare and dun brown as it was now, and so vast.

And Kunnunurra had enchanted her, all six hundred acres of it and the comfortable old house up on the hill with its white-fenced garden and trees, its myriad birds, its peace and tranquillity on a hot summer's day when the view shimmered in a heat haze; the cosy retreat it offered in winter from the wind and the rain.

'But now it all frightens me,' she murmured and shivered, but not from the chilly air.

'Mum?' Matt said.

Kate turned to see that he was watching her with a slight frown.

'Is something wrong? You looked . . . funny.'

'No, love,' she said with a smile and rubbed his cold nose with her forefinger. 'Oh, that looks much better!'

The sign was now nailed on straight.

'Tell you what, I think we ought to paint it. It's nearly faded away.'

'Oh, can I, Mum?' Matt said enthusiastically.

'Yes, you can. But not today—we might leave that for another day.'

'Dark blue would look nice, don't you think?' Matt said. 'And it would stand out, wouldn't it?'

'Yes it would. I wonder if we've got any? But anyway, let's get home now before Serena starts to worry. In you hop. No, not *you,* you disreputable hound. Digby! Into the back with you! I refuse to be slobbered all over.'

Later that night, when Matt and his twin sister Serena were in bed and fast asleep, Kate stared into the fire she'd built up to last all night, and thought, I don't know why I didn't fix the mail box days ago . . . The truth is, the whole place is falling apart and so am I. Perhaps they were right, all those people who said a woman couldn't cope with a property like this?

'On the other hand,' she murmured, 'what am I to do? The market is supposedly depressed and even if I could find a buyer I'd get back barely sufficient to pay off the mortgage—and I'd have nothing. At least this way we have a roof over our heads and some sort of an income. Oh, Mike, why did you have to die and leave me?'

She dropped her head into her hands and couldn't stop herself from thinking back.

The only daughter of a solicitor, she had been born in Toowoomba, a city in status but in reality more of a big country town that served the Downs and was perched picturesquely on the edge of the Great Dividing Range. At school, she had mixed with the daughters of many grain growers, and of graziers from further outback, and had spent several holidays on properties out west, always dreaming of living on one herself.

No one had been more surprised at the manner in which she had achieved this than she had been.

She had dearly loved her quiet, absent-minded father who had never remarried after Kate's mother had died, and had had extremely old-fashioned views on women. This had led him to insist that his only daughter got a good grounding in home economics, that she take a child-care course and that she learn to play the piano—the last being his ultimate concept of femininity, apparently. And when she had finished school, he had taken her on a grand tour of Europe where he'd attended to her artistic and cultural development and appreciation personally. If it had ever occurred to him that his lithe, vibrant daughter, with her sometimes impulsive nature, was simply not fashioned in the mould of his concept of a 'lady', which was something delicate and passive and unfailingly sweet, he had ignored the thought and had insisted that she work for him in his office for at least a year after they had returned from Europe.

And despite the fact that Kate had secretly seen herself as a much more modern woman and had had visions of pursuing a variety of exciting careers, she had acquiesced—for a year. By then his health hadn't been too good.

Only, well before the year had ended, an angry young man had stormed into the office one day, bent on extracting legal retribution over the matter of an inheritance, and had fallen in love with Kate on sight. Three months later she had married Mike Wiley with not the slightest qualm about all the exciting careers she was passing up, her father had sorted out Mike's inheritance problems, which had freed a monetary bequest from his grandfather, they'd put a deposit on Kunnunurra and, with some additional help from Kate's father, had moved in. Thus fulfilling her early dreams and Mike's burning ambition to become a farmer. The land had always fascinated him, too, and he'd studied agriculture at the Gatton College.

They had had four blissful years, although her father had died early on in the marriage. But Kate liked to think that he had died happy about her marriage and her life, although she'd been unable to hide from him that she actually enjoyed helping Mike more and more and had become quite proficient at driving tractors and all aspects of farm life that were not essentially feminine. And after his death she had put her inheritance into Kununnurra to reduce the mortgage.

But despite her handiness in other things, when the twins were born she had discovered herself possessed of a flood of maternal instincts, too. Life couldn't have been better . . .

Then life had fallen apart. A freak trailer accident had taken Mike from her just before the twins' fourth birthday and the agony of it had been unbelievable. And, as if that wasn't bad enough, the year leading up to it had not been a good one, either. Drought had seen them lose several valuable crops and, without Mike, Kate had suddenly been made painfully aware of her financial obligations, too, and had seen Mike's life insurance slip through her fingers like a drop in the ocean.

How she'd battled on, she never knew. Why she'd battled on had been clearer to her. In memory of a beloved husband, mainly, but also because she'd discovered that she didn't like to be beaten at anything.

Up until now she had been able to meet her mortgage obligations, but only just. For one thing she had had to sub-contract out her ploughing, planting and harvesting—there had been no way she could have done it herself—but it had increased costs dramatically. Then she had had a run-in with a mystery disease to barley.

'But how long will I be able to keep going?' she asked herself, coming back to the present with a sigh. 'It's getting *harder* every year instead of easier. And what say we have another drought, or flood, or pestilence or . . . God knows what!'

She stared miserably into the fire for ages; then, realising it was past midnight, she took herself off to bed.

10 Consequently, having sat up so late, Kate felt less inclined than ever to cope with things the next morning, and nothing went right from the start . . .

'Mum, Matt and I need new clothes,' Serena said very seriously over breakfast the next morning. 'Everything is getting too small.'

'We're shooting up, aren't we?' Matt said.

'I'm afraid you are,' Kate agreed with an inward sigh. 'I'll be going in to Toowoomba next week. I'll see what I can do.'

'Can I come, too?' Serena asked.

'I was . . . ' Kate broke off and bit her lip. Going to go to the second-hand shop, she'd been about to say, but Serena looked so expectant at the prospect of some *new* clothes, she just didn't have the heart. 'All right, we'll make it a Saturday morning,' she said instead and was rewarded by a dazzling smile from her daughter. Serena was beautiful, a beautiful little girl with long dark silky hair and blue eyes. She was also essentially feminine and really enjoyed pottering around the house, and would have been a joy to her grandfather's heart.

As for her twin, who was the younger by about ten minutes, he was looking more like his father every day, Kate thought. Mike had had the very dark hair and blue eyes while her own hair was a glossy chestnut, normally, and her eyes a clear, luminous grey.

'What's that?' Kate said to Serena. 'Sorry, I was dreaming.'

'I said, there's a new kid at school in our class. I don't like him.'

'I do. He's all right!' Matt said.

'That's because you're a boy,' Serena retorted. 'And because he let you use his baseball mitt. But I think he's too full of himself by half. Who cares if his father is the richest man around here anyway?' She tossed her head.

'*He* didn't say that,' Matt reproved. 'Stanley Watson said it. But it's true.'

'Kids, don't squabble,' Kate said. 'Who is he?'

'Thomas Robertson the Third,' Serena said, rolling her eyes and giggling.

'The Third? Oh, you mean . . . ' Kate frowned.

'Uh-huh. Eton,' Serena said. 'They've moved in. But I don't care if he's the Third or . . . '

'He's only the Third because his father and grandfather are called Thomas . . .   Well, his grandfather's dead now and anyway his father . . .   Mum,' Matt said exasperatedly, 'tell her to stop making faces at me. She doesn't like him because he pulled her hair, but . . . '

'That could be a fair reason not to like someone.' Kate suggested.

'But it was a dare and it was only Serena because she gets so mad, but Tom didn't know that. She knocked Stanley Watson cold once.'

Kate blinked.

'I did not! I slapped his face,' Serena said haughtily. 'And he deserved it!'

'But why?' Kate enquired, finding herself on a chilly winter's morning unexpectedly revising her opinions of her daughter—is she more like me than I imagined?

'He said we were so poor we had to eat the flies off the wall, and that we were ruining a good property and that it shouldn't be allowed. So I slapped him,' Serena said casually. 'You would have done the same anyway, Matt.'

Matt agreed ruefully.

Kate stared at them both with narrowed eyes. The Watson property was five miles down the road and the ubiquitous Stanley Watson's father was a shire councillor. Kate could just picture Les Watson—a male chauvinist extraordinaire she'd always thought, anyway—uttering those sentiments, obviously often enough for his son Stanley to have learned them off pat.

'It's not true, is it, Mum?' Serena asked then.

'Well,' Kate said with an effort, 'we're certainly not eating the flies off the wall, are we?' she parried and jumped up. 'I'd just ignore that kind of talk, kids. It's no one's business but our own and when we get our next grain cheque, we'll be able to do some improvements. Now, we'll have to sprint to get through the chores before the school bus comes, so let's look lively.'

They had an arrangement on school mornings that Serena helped Kate with the house while Matt fed and watered the domestic stock—a rather grand term to apply to one horse, six turkeys, a dozen or so chickens and one extremely naughty goat. And a dog and a cat.

Fortunately, the old wooden house wasn't very big and, despite needing a coat of paint on the outside, was compact and basically modernised within. Mike had done the renovations in the first year of their marriage and had proved a whizz at restoring old furniture, so it was lovingly furnished, comfortable and one of the few sources of consolation Kate seemed to have these days.

It was always a relief, especially in winter, to come into the snug lounge with its open fireplace, or the kitchen which doubled as a dining-room with its cheerful red-tiled floor and enormous old Welsh dresser that housed her collection of fine china.

But it was ages since she'd gone searching for china, Kate thought dismally as she dusted her collection that morning.

Serena was at the kitchen sink, singing cheerfully as she washed the breakfast dishes.

'OK, love,' Kate said after watching her for some moments unobserved, 'I'll finish off. Time to go for the bus. Give Matt a yell, will you?'

She watched them trudging down the drive a few minutes later, bundled up against a freezing westerly but cheerful enough to have a little shoving match as they went, and her heart felt like bursting with love and pride. They were two kids in a million, she was sure, and Mike would have been so proud of them—and Les Watson could go to hell!

It was only as she was putting the washing on that she remembered their news about Thomas Robertson—the Third.

'So they've arrived,' she said to herself as she sorted through the pile of clothes. 'I'm surprised Marcie hasn't been up to fill me in. I expect Eton is all set to take up its rightful position as the showcase of the district once more.'

Eton, named presumably after the most famous of the great playing fields of England, was undoubtedly the most famous property in the district. And not only for its size, which made Kunnunurra look like a pocket handkerchief, but for its beautiful old colonial homestead and the fact that, until recently, it had been owned by the descendants of the family that had pioneered the area. But the Morcambe family had finally run out and, twelve months ago, Eton, a smaller property near Warwick and the Morcambe's Toowoomba residence had come on to the open market.

There had been much speculation in the district as to who would buy Eton, and some surprise when the purchasers had turned out to be another pioneering family, the Robertsons. Surprise because the Robertsons had always been graziers as opposed to grain growers, with a far-flung empire of cattle properties in western and central Queensland—a very different thing to the Darling Downs. But, if anything, the Robertson family went back even further than the Morcambes had in the 'squatocracy' stakes, and a pleasurable buzz of speculation had settled on the district. The Robertsons had put in a manager, however, and eventually most people had come to doubt that the family itself would ever take up Eton as their residence—a crying shame, many had thought wistfully. After all, it was such a beautiful house and setting and what could they possibly have out beyond the black stump to equal it?

Kate herself had had more than enough to worry her without bothering about the comings and goings of the Robertson family, although Kunnunurra did share a common boundary with Eton for about half a mile along a western corner. But she had remembered that Mike had once told her briefly of how he'd come to save the life of a member of that family during his days as a representative for a stock and station agency.

He had been travelling between Quilpie and Thargomindah, way, way out west, on a burningly hot day, and had come suddenly upon the wreck of a car with the driver unconscious in it and a dead, stray bullock beside it. And he had told her how he'd judged that it had only just happened and how he had smelt petrol and dragged the unconscious driver out, only moments before the petrol had ignited and the car had gone up in flames.

'But that was . . . What was the name?' Kate murmured, thinking of it again and smiling to herself as she remembered how Mike had clammed up after telling her about this deed of heroism. Especially after she had pointed out that he could have been incinerated and must have known it after he had smelt petrol. 'Um, something unusual . . . ' She closed the lid of the washing machine and twirled a knob absent-mindedly. 'Graham . . . No, *Grevil,* that's it. Anyway, not

Thomas, so he must have been a younger son or a cousin.'

She twirled the knob again, staring at it but not seeing it, then it suddenly dawned on her that nothing was happening—no sound of water pouring in, nothing. She checked that the wall plug was switched on, which it was, so she switched it off, pulled the plug out and pushed it back into the socket carefully, but still nothing happened when she switched on again. She checked the taps, conscious of a rising flood of annoyance and help-lessness. 'Work, damn you!' she exhorted it, twirling knobs again, but to no avail. Nor did the solid kick she gave the casing achieve anything.

'Well, that's just about it!' she shouted at it, and with a hand to her mouth whirled around and ran through the kitchen to her bedroom to fling herself on to the bed and indulge in a bout of desperate tears.

Some time later she sat up and rubbed her face wearily and contemplated the fact that she would have to go cap in hand yet again to her bank manager because she was just not going to last until her grain cheque came—that much was obvious. Getting anything fixed this far out of town was hideously expensive and who was to say it was fixable anyway? An eight-year-old washing machine that had been bought second hand in the first place? On the other hand, the thought of going through winter having to wash by hand was just the last straw. And she had promised the kids new clothes. Oh, God, what am I going to do? she entreated. I'm already in hock for so much of that cheque . . . What am I going to do?

But God emulated the washing machine and it was the sound of a powerful motor that disturbed her agonised reverie.

Kate glanced out of her bedroom window to see a large, unfamiliar maroon Range Rover slam to a dusty halt outside the garden gate. She watched with a morbid kind of fascination as a strange man strode through the gate, waved his hat at Digby and Billy the goat—who was insatiably curious—so that they both retreated smartly, then paused to look around.

With Technicolor clarity, a vision of what he was seeing swept through Kate's mind. The cracked, weed-choked tennis court with its high mesh sagging in places, the unmown lawn that had taken over most of the flower beds, the roses which had once been her pride and joy but were now over-grown and needing pruning . . .

If he had shouted it from the rooftops, the stranger standing in the middle of her garden could not have expressed his disgust more clearly than he did with a movement of his wide shoulders.

'Who does he think he is?' Kate muttered, sitting up straighter, her grey eyes glittering suddenly.

Then he disappeared from view on to the front porch, and she frowned and hesitated slightly before going to answer his knock.

For some odd reason, neither of them spoke as she opened the door. Well, not so odd really, she was to think later; whatever else you like to think about him, that first impact is quite something.

For one thing she hadn't realised how tall he was until she was standing in front of him. And she was about five foot ten herself. But he was obviously well over six foot, with a magnificent body, those wide shoulders encased in a khaki bush shirt and brown sweater, tapering to a taut torso, lean hips and long legs in dusty jeans.

Kate's startled gaze flickered upwards again and she found herself staring into a tanned face possessing a well-cut mouth and a pair of hazel eyes with green flecks in them beneath thick fairish hair. She also noticed that he had a slight tendency to freckles . . .

It was at that point that she realised she was staring at this prime example of masculinity open-mouthed, as if she'd never seen a good-looking man before. She shut her mouth with some inward disgust and, as her teeth clicked together, she realised something else: that she was being comprehensively summed up from head to toe and, moreover, comprehensively dismissed in a way that no female of the species could misunderstand. But what was worse, in a reflex action she looked downwards herself, at her baggy old tracksuit trousers and shabby sandshoes, her shapeless jumper, her red, rough hands—and she didn't have to see her face to know that her skin was dry and her hair lifeless and dull.

She caught her breath, furious with herself and this mocking stranger, and said sharply, 'Who the hell are you?'

He lifted an eyebrow and drawled, 'We haven't met yet, Mrs Riley, but . . . '

'I know that!' she interrupted. 'Nor do I really want to change it,' she added, not quite beneath her breath. 'So will you please state your business. I haven't got time to stand around chatting,' she said briskly and with as much hauteur as she could manage.

The stranger narrowed his hazel eyes and surveyed her in silence for a moment. Then he said deliberately, 'Very well. That straggly bunch of steers you own, Mrs Riley, broke through your equally straggly fence last night and cut a swathe through my oats paddock big enough to accommodate the Sydney Opera House.'

Kate had opened her mouth to say *Wiley,* not Riley, but she closed it, and paled.

'Quite,' the man said coolly and folded his arms across his chest. 'Now, you obviously have problems—that much I can see—but I believe it is your obligation to keep that fence in order.'

'Which . . . one is that?' Kate asked, but with a sudden, sinking certainty.

'Your boundary with Eton,' the man said and waved away a fly with one long, strong hand.

'Oh . . . ' Kate put a hand to her mouth and closed her eyes briefly. Then she stiffened her spine and said proudly, 'I'm sorry. I wasn't aware the fence was unsafe but I'll attend to it immediately. Good day.'

'Hang on,' the man said idly, but putting out that lean hand to stop her closing the door in his face. 'What about my oats?'

Kate had a short sharp struggle with the door during which she got very red in the face, he gave the impression he could hold up the Bank of England with one hand, and the door remained open.

'What about them?' she cried, suddenly enraged as well as humiliated. 'It was accidental. It's the first time I've been negligent over fences, so good riddance to your flaming oats! In case you don't know it, Mr Thomas Robertson the Second—and I presume that's who you are—you have enough oats on Eton to feed the nation! And by the way, it sounds as if your son is growing up to be just as big-headed as you are!'

And she took the opportunity, as a flicker of surprise at this onslaught crossed his even features and he shifted his weight, to do it this time: close the door on him smartly and lean back against it, trembling from head to toe.

Then, in the grip of what she later recognised as hysterical reaction, she flung the door open again and spat at him, 'And it's *Wiley,* not Riley!' She didn't even bother to close the door this time, but stalked away from it and into the kitchen.

It wasn't until she heard his footsteps going down the front steps and the Range Rover driving away that she began to ponder the unwisdom if not insanity of her behaviour. And she burst into tears.

It took a cup of tea to restore her to some kind of watery composure.

'I was in the wrong,' she told herself, as she sipped her tea at the kitchen table and stared out over the back garden towards the water tank. 'Nothing alters that—not even the fact that he looked at me like a sultan recruiting for his harem. It is my fence and it's my duty to restrain my stock. I expect, if he decided to sue me, I'd have to pay compensation.'

The prospect of this was so horrifying, she poured herself some more tea and added a tot of rum to it.

But not only that, she went on to think dismally, in the space of a few short minutes I've completely alienated, I'm sure, a very powerful person in the district. He'll probably end up shire chairman like the Morcambes always did. Oh, hell!

She stared unseeingly over the back garden again, oblivious to the fact that the goat was chewing up an old sack for lack of anything more destructive to do. It had been the twins' pet as a kid and perfectly sweet then.

'The least I can do is fix the fence,' Kate said and sighed.

Fencing was not her favourite occupation but she had all the right tools and had achieved a degree of proficiency at it, provided she didn't have to put in posts. So it was some relief to see that the posts in the west paddock were sound; it was just the wiring that had rusted and weakened and come down. It was also with some relief that she saw her 'straggly' mob of steers on the the right side of the fence.

'It's barbed wire for you lot,' she yelled at them as she drove past. 'And talk about a last supper! I'm getting rid of you whether beef prices rise or not!'

Actually they weren't that straggly and, following Mike's practice, she annually went to the cattle sales, bought some weanlings, fattened them up for six months or so, then sold them—generally making a profit because it cost nothing to feed them on her good, nourishing grass. This year, however, beef prices had tumbled and she doubted whether she'd get what she paid for them.

'Just my luck,' she muttered gloomily, still sitting in the cab of the ute, reluctant to leave its relative warmth. But finally she pulled on her balaclava, her padded jacket and thick working gloves and stepped out into the wind.

Although it was only one section of the fence that was down, it took her all morning to restrand it and strain it. It was a back-breaking, hand-hurting job but, when she finally finished, the strands were taut and well secured. Then she walked the rest of it, testing it carefully and hoping to God it would hold. Having once got through, her mob of steers would be doubly persistent now, she knew. She was tempted to herd them into another paddock just to be on the safe side, but knew she wouldn't have the energy. I should have done that first, she thought wearily. I really am losing my touch. She glanced resentfully across the fence, but there was no sign of life on Eton, so she packed up her tools and drove home with a heavy heart.

There was a small red car outside the garden fence and as Kate drove the ute into the shed, a petite brunette jumped out of it.

'Knew you'd be around somewhere,' Marcie Hunter, who was Kate's best friend, greeted her as she came out of the shed.

'You should have gone in!' Kate said affectionately. 'Come in now, anyway. Have you had lunch?'

'No, I was hoping you'd offer me some.' Marcie's green eyes twinkled. But she added anxiously, 'What on earth have you been doing? You look exhausted!'

Kate told her as she led the way inside and peeled off her gloves. 'I think I'm going to have blisters.'

'Oh, Kate!' Marcie looked slightly shocked as she inspected Kate's hands. 'You sit down,' she said firmly then. 'I'll make lunch. What's it to be?'

'I made some soup yesterday—it only needs heating and we could have toast.'

'Done! Why don't you get some salve for your hands?'

It was later, when they were having a cup of coffee, that Marcie said suddenly, 'Kate, I'm worried about you.'

Kate eyed her friend over the top of her cup. Marcie was married to the head teacher of the local school and, perhaps because they had both arrived in the district at the same time as brides, they had formed a bond of special friendship. Although such was Marcie's disposition, most people were her friends. But it did go deeper than that between them, Kate knew, just as she knew that, without Marcie, she might have given up ages ago and that it had been Marcie alone who had managed to break through the wall of grief and pain she had felt when Mike had died.

She sighed suddenly and put her cup down. 'I am falling apart, aren't I? It's strange. I thought the first couple of years were bound to be the worst and up until a few months ago, I really thought I was coping. Oh, not brilliantly, but—coping. Now I feel as if every step I take is like walking through heavy water.'

'You're trying to do too much. You have been for years,' Marcie said intensely. 'For heaven's sake, you're only a woman!'

A glimmer of a smile briefly lit Kate's grey eyes. Marcie was well known for her views on the equality of the sexes. But what she said next really took Kate by surprise.

'Also, you need a man.'

Kate blinked and Marcie tilted her chin. 'You must be lonely, Kate,' she said softly then.

Kate stood up restlessly. 'I've got Matt and Serena,' she said after a moment.

'You know what I mean. It's been four years now and I knew Mike and I'm sure he wouldn't have expected you to spend the rest of your life on your own! But you refuse to even go to the local socials . . . '

'I know every man around for miles,' Kate interrupted wearily. 'Anyway, I have it on good authority that I might not be able to get myself a man—supposing I wanted one, which . . . '

'Who told you that? Of all the nerve!'

Kate smiled. 'I thought so, too,' she said ruefully. 'But maybe it's a case of the truth hurting . . . ' She stopped and bit her lip and wondered with a curious little pang how true *that* was.

'Kate,' Marcie said ominously, 'don't you dare clam up on me now. Who was it?'

'Well, he didn't actually say it,' Kate hedged and glanced at Marcie who was wearing an unusually militant and stubborn expression. She sighed. 'It was Thomas Robertson—Thomas Two; I believe there have been three.'

Marcie's mouth dropped open. 'You've met him?'

'Not only met him, but that's why I was mending fences this morning.' She crossed to the stove and poured herself another cup of coffee.

'Oh, tell me about him,' Marcie begged. 'Roy met him when he enrolled his kid at school but you know what Roy's like,' she said of her quiet, scholarly husband. 'All I could get him to say was that he seemed a good sort of a bloke. Describe him!'

Kate thought for a bit and decided she'd rather not, but another glance at Marcie's expectant face told her she was going to have to come up with the goods. 'Late thirties, maybe forty, very tall, darkish fair hair, if you know what I mean, well built . . . ' She pondered for a moment. 'And very, very sure of himself.'

'And you didn't like him?'

'No. He reminded me of King Solomon.'

Marcie giggled. 'He sounds divine, if you ask me.'

Kate grimaced and told her friend what had happened. 'If he hadn't looked at me like that I wouldn't have said what I did—I don't think. But he just totally rubbed me up the wrong way. Only, I was already in the wrong.'

Marcie pursed her lips. 'Awkward,' she commented. 'Perhaps he didn't understand how you're placed?'

'I think he did. I mean, he didn't ask for the man of the house so he must have known there was none. And I think on the whole people are becoming less understanding about it, Marcie.' She related what Les Watson's child had said to Serena.

'I wouldn't worry about Les Watson,' Marcie said arctically. 'Anyway, it's none of his business!'

'Unfortunately it becomes his business, as a shire councillor, when I get behind with my weed control programme, which I did last summer. Marcie,' Kate sat down dispiritedly, 'I think I'm going to have to face facts soon. The last thing Mike would have wanted was for me to become a liability on the whole district. I think I'll just have to put the place on the market, get what I can for it and then head for town and try and get a job.'

'What kind of a job?'

'Anything.'

'What about your grain cheque?'

'At the rate I'm going, there'll be none left.'

'Is there no way,' Marcie said very seriously, 'that you could take a break? Just a few days—Matt and Serena could come and stay with us. Pete would love to have them.' Pete was her seven-year-old son.

Kate chewed her lip. 'I can't leave the place unattended even if I could afford it,' she said at last. 'God knows what might happen. But thanks all the same,' she added warmly. 'And don't worry about me, promise? Who knows, a miracle might occur overnight!'

Marcie looked unconvinced, but she smiled.

By the time the school bus arrived, Kate had bathed and changed and was looking more presentable. The least I can do is not infect the kids with my gloom, she thought, and whipped up a batch of pikelets.

She heard them coming up the drive and immediately detected a strange voice, but it was not unusual for Matt or Serena to bring a friend home to play so she didn't pay much attention until they burst into the kitchen and the friend turned out to be a perfectly strange little boy with an engagingly freckled face and a wide grin.

'Well, who have we here?' she enquired.

'This is Tom Robertson, Mum,' Matt said. 'He's come to spend the afternoon.'

CHAPTER TWO

KATE froze.

'How do you do, Mrs Wiley,' Tom Robertson said politely. 'I hope you don't mind. Matt said you wouldn't.'

'*I* mind,' Serena muttered somewhat darkly and stalked through to her room.

Masters Tom and Matt exchanged amused glances.

'Well,' Kate said, loosening her tongue, 'no, but we do have some rules around here, Tom.'

'Oh, it's all right, Mum,' Matt said earnestly. 'We asked Marcie—Mrs Hunter—if we could ring Tom's dad. Actually she did it for us.'

'Marcie spoke . . . ' Oh, Marcie, Kate thought, just you wait until . . .

'Yes, she spoke to Mr Robertson, Mum, and told him Tom and me had made friends. He said that was fine and he would pick him up at six.'

Kate all but choked. 'Your father said that?' She couldn't help looking incredulous.

'That's what Mrs Hunter said,' Tom said very seriously. 'She had a bit of a chat with Dad, she said, but I knew he'd be happy that I've found a friend.'

'Oh.' Kate looked at the two eager faces in front of her. 'Well, it is nice,' she said lamely.

' 'Specially as Tom is like us, Mum,' Matt said. 'He hasn't got a mother, so . . . '

'Haven't you, Tom?'

'No. She died when I was little, but . . . '

'Oh wow! Pikelets,' Matt interrupted. 'Do you like 'em, Tom?'

'Love them! They're my favourite tea.'

This was said so glowingly that Kate couldn't help smiling faintly, and thinking that Serena might have been wrong about this Thomas.

'Well, sit down, boys. Er, by the way, I hope you don't intend to torment the life out of Serena this afternoon.'

'I said I was sorry for pulling her hair, Mrs Wiley. It was a dare, you see, on my first day.' Tom rolled his eyes. 'You do some silly things on your first day.'

And I do silly things whatever the day, Kate thought bitterly. How on earth am I going to face your father later? 'Well,' she said helplessly, 'I'm sure she'll get over it. Milk or juice, boys?'

During the course of the afternoon, several possibilities presented themselves to Kate. She could, for example, drop Tom off home herself, a bit earlier and with some excuse about having somewhere to go. But that would mean awkward, not to say untruthful, explanations to Matt. And she did think of manufacturing some emergency in a distant paddock, but then she always made it a rule never to leave other people's children unattended. And anyway, what had Marcie said to the man? Knowing her, she probably told him my whole sad story, thought Kate. *Marcie*—I know, I'll ring *you!*

But there was no one home at the Hunter house which adjoined the small, three-teacher schoolhouse.

'Damn!' Kate put the phone down and stared at it frustratedly.

In the end she did nothing.

At half past five she went to find the children because it was nearly dark and very cold. Serena had finally shed her chilly reserve, and they were playing an energetic game of tag behind the stables.

As Kate walked back with the three of them tagging along at a distance, she saw the maroon Range Rover parked at the fence and Thomas Robertson leaning on the garden gate.

She hesitated then walked over to him. 'It's O.K. He's quite safe,' she said. 'I haven't vented my ill-humour on him. And I believe I owe you an apology.'

They looked at each other in the half light and Thomas Robertson straightened slowly. He said, 'That's all right, Mrs Wiley. I don't normally carry my squabbles down to eight-year-olds either.'

Kate bit her lip and looked away uncertainly. Then the kids rushed up and Tom was telling his father what a great time he'd had but it wasn't even six o'clock yet!

'Tom,' Kate said, 'your dad might have other things to do, so . . .'

'Actually, I came early because I'd like to have a word with you, Mrs Wiley,' Tom's father interrupted.

'I . . .'

'Oh, great!' Matt enthused, 'we've got some more time. Come inside, Tom!' And the three of them raced in, leaving Kate no choice but to say awkwardly, 'Very well. Shall we go in, too?'

The children had occupied the kitchen table so Kate led the way into the lounge, where she already had a fire going, and closed the door.

Turning to her unexpected guest abruptly, she said, 'I feel I owe you an explanation as well as an apology, Mr Robertson. I said some unforgivable things this morning—your son is a very nice little boy, in fact.' She trailed off uncomfortably and thought she detected a gleam of amusement in those hazel eyes.

'How kind of you to say so, Mrs Wiley,' he murmured, and waited.

'I also . . . well . . . ' Kate went on nervously but determinedly, 'should not have implied the things about you that I did, and I probably wouldn't have if the washing machine hadn't just broken down on me and you hadn't . . . ' she paused, then decided to be absolutely honest, 'hadn't rather made me aware of the mess I was in—am in. And,' she drew a quivering breath, 'if you've come to see me about compensation for your oats, I'm sorry but I'm just not in the position to . . . ' She stopped and looked down at her raw, blistered hands which she was rubbing together agitatedly, and for some unaccountable reason thrust them behind her back. ' . . . to pay you anything at present, but with a bit of time, well . . . ' She shrugged.

He said nothing for a moment, then, 'You know as well as I do that's highly unlikely.'

'What—what did you want to speak me about then?' Kate whispered and cleared her throat.

She was still standing at the door and he was standing in the middle of the room but he walked across towards her, only stopping when he was right in front of her. Kate stared up at him with her eyes wide and wary and found she felt like turning and running away for some reason. And she realised suddenly that it was a long time since she'd met a man who was so intimidating.

But she stood her ground and he smiled slightly as if guessing her dilemma, and said, 'I came to compliment you on your fencing, for one thing.' And taking her by surprise, he reached behind her for one of her hands which he inspected closely. 'But you've made a mess of these, haven't you?' he added mildly.

Kate stared at her hand lying in his tanned one and felt a curious prickle of awareness travel right up her arm, which had the effect of making her snatch her hand away and of feeling illogically angry.

'Then why——If that's true, why did you let me go on grovelling like that?' she asked indignantly.

He laughed. '*You* had the last word this morning if you recall, Mrs Wiley,' he said lazily.

Kate's nostrils flared and the look she cast him should have stunned one of her steers. But it only caused Thomas Robertson the Second further amusement, and caused him to say, 'Are you always this hot-tempered? Or has another disaster befallen you since I was last here?'

With a great effort of will, Kate restrained her unruly tongue and temper, and wondered briefly what it was about this man that got to her so. Then a look of confusion clouded her grey eyes and she bit her lip helplessly.

He said, after watching her for some moments, 'Perhaps we ought to start again, Mrs Wiley. Let's erase this morning. I'm Grevil Robertson. How do you do?'

Kate's mouth dropped open. '*You're* the one Mike saved?' she said in stunned accents.

Those lazy hazel eyes regarded her narrowly. 'And you are the wife of the Mike Wiley who pulled me out of a wrecked car moments before it blew up, I believe. I wondered as soon as I got the name right.'

'Widow,' she whispered. 'But I thought you were Thomas . . . '

'I am. But I've always been known by my second name to avoid confusion with my father—and now my son. So Mike told you all about it?'

'He mentioned it once, that's all.'

'And you never thought this morning that I might have been the recipient of that great favour?'

'I . . . No. Well, I *was* thinking about it this morning, funnily enough, just before the washing machine gave up the ghost. Because the kids had brought it up at breakfast, you see.' She recounted that conversation and added lamely, 'That's how I got the wrong impression of your son. Serena, well, objected to having her hair pulled but she's obviously forgiven him.' Kate smiled weakly. 'And I assumed that Mike's *Grevil* Robertson must have been someone else, a brother or a cousin.'

'They're very much like their father, aren't they?' Grevil Robertson said quietly. 'I could see it straight away. I don't think I'll ever forget Mike Wiley's face.'

Kate blinked away a tear. 'Yes, they are . . . '

'Mrs Wiley . . . may I call you Kate?'

'How . . . ?' Kate tried to swallow her tears.

'How do I know it's Kate? I had a telephone conversation this afternoon with a lady I've never met but she filled me in on certain details. You're in dire straits, aren't you, Kate?'

Kate closed her eyes briefly. 'Marcie shouldn't have done that—only Marcie *would!*'

'She said you were her best friend and that you were nearly at the end of your tether otherwise she was quite sure you would never have reacted the way you did this morning. She said she only knew about it because she'd come to lunch, but as soon as Tom and Matt had come to her to ask if they could ring me up, she had perceived a way in which she might be able to sort things out. She was extremely persuasive,' he said wryly. 'I should imagine most people would count themselves lucky to have her as a friend.'

Kate licked her lips. 'I *do,* but it's no one's business but my own.'

'That was something I thought we might discuss.'

Kate's heart started to hammer, she discovered. 'I don't know what you mean . . . ' She broke off in confusion.

'I thought there might be a way I could help.'

'No. No I couldn't accept charity,' she said dazedly.

'Who said anything about charity?' he enquired with a quirk of his eyebrows.

'You said *help.*'

'And I meant help, assistance—something like Mike Wiley gave *me* once when I was in dire straits.'

'He . . . he wouldn't have expected to be *repaid* for that,' she stammered.

'No. He made that very clear at the time,' Grevil Robertson murmured. 'On the other hand, if our positions had been reversed, I don't suppose he'd have stood by and watched my family go through these hard times if he was able to help?'

'But you don't understand. I'm in so deep now I could never repay you,' Kate said desperately. 'It would only be a waste of your . . . help, and I'd be beholden to you for ever. Anyone else who'd come along would have done the same as Mike, anyway. It was just one of those things. I . . . ' She took a breath. 'Thank you very much for the offer but I honestly think I'm best to cut my losses now.'

He was silent for a time, then he said, 'There are two other people involved, aren't there? Mike's children. Shouldn't you consider them before you fling my offer back in my face?'

'I'm not *flinging* anything. I'm . . . ' She put a hand to her mouth.

He said drily. 'Then it must be something personal.'

Kate's eyes fell away from his direct, faintly mocking hazel gaze and a tinge of colour rose in her cheeks. But before she could answer, a crash came from the kitchen and a moment's dead silence then some muffled squeaks of laughter before Serena called out, 'It's all right, Mum. Nothing's broken!'

Grevil Robertson smiled. 'Sounds as if they're getting a bit overexcited.'

'Yes. It does,' Kate agreed.

'Tell you what, I think I'll take Tom home now. But I'd like you to think this over tonight. I guess it's come as a bit of a surprise to you.'

Kate turned away from those rather acute hazel eyes.

'Yes, it has.' she agreed lamely, and thought he laughed, but when she turned back he was regarding her quite seriously. 'But I . . . ' she began.

'No,' he interrupted. 'We'll discuss it again in the morning. *Au revoir,* Mrs Wiley. Thank you very much for having Tom.'

'Oh, *that* was a pleasure . . . ' Kate broke off and bit her lip.

Before she went to bed, Kate stood in the middle of her bedroom, still feeling stunned and bewildered. And she thought of Mike who had saved Grevil Robertson's life, of Mike who had loved her so . . .

She wandered over to her dressing-table and picked up the silver-framed wedding photo that stood on it. And when her eyes lifted to her reflection in the mirror they were shimmering with tears. For the face in the photo was so young and carefree and happy, so different to the face she saw in the mirror.

She had worn her thick, straight chestnut hair very long then and Mike had loved that. But then Mike had loved every inch of her, or so he had said—her slender, yet, in the right places, opulent figure, her smooth skin, the fringe of dark lashes about her grey eyes that had been, actually still were, she thought, luxuriously thick, her widow's peak that made her face heart-shaped, her wide generous mouth. And he'd loved her sense of fun and adventure, although he'd often teased her about tormenting the life out of him. Perhaps I did, she thought, but I always knew when to give in— *you* always knew how to make me give in and love it. Oh, Mike, what shall I do? You were always so certain this was the kind of life you wanted your children to have and I know how hard it would be for them to adjust to city life and a mother who was never there—that's assuming I could get a job. If I couldn't we'd have to exist on the pension and that might send me round the bend. On the other hand how can I accept anything from a complete stranger?

'One I don't even particularly like?' she murmured aloud. 'No, it's impossible. Besides, a sum of money is only going to tide me over.'

She put the photo down and wandered around the room restlessly, and found herself wondering why she didn't particularly like Grevil Robertson. After what had transpired when he had come to pick Tom up, she should have been able to reverse her opinion, surely?

'Any normal person would have. Wouldn't they?' She stopped in front of her dressing-table again and put the question to her reflection in the mirror. The answer that popped into her mind amazed her a little.

'You're still smarting from that *look* he gave you this morning, aren't you, Kate?' she asked herself softly. 'Well, why shouldn't I be?' she went on, standing up straighter suddenly and squaring her shoulders. 'I'm a *person,* aren't I? And I should be judged as one, *not* on how desirable I might be to the opposite sex. I hate that kind of thing.

But as she studied herself, her shoulders slumped again and she turned away and sat down on the bed dismally. On the other hand—not that it's any of Grevil Robertson's business—I have let myself go lately, she admitted to herself. I just don't seem to have the time or the inclination or the energy or the money to bother. But perhaps worst of all, no inclination . . .

He came at about eleven the next morning.

It was a wet, windy day, but not quite so cold. Kate invited him into the kitchen and offered him coffee. He looked around the bright, cheerful room and accepted, and she made the coffee in silence while he inspected her china.

'You have quite a collection,' he said as she poured the coffee.

'Yes. I've been fascinated by china and porcelain ever since I visited some of the factories in Europe.'

'Was that with Mike?'

'Mike——No, my father took me overseas after I left school. Mr Robertson . . . '

'Grevil,' he said. 'Do call me Grevil.'

She hesitated. He was dressed differently today, in a pair of brown cord trousers, a checked sports shirt open at the throat and a magnificent soft leather jacket. And his fairish hair was tamed and tidy. He looked, she thought briefly, anything but a farmer, as if he could take his place amongst sophisticated city dwellers with ease. In fact she had taken some trouble with *her* appearance, resolutely quashing an inner voice which had queried quietly whether she wasn't kowtowing to that *look*. I just need to acquire some confidence in dealing with this man, she'd told herself. So, with luck, confidence had been donned along with a pair of faded but well pressed blue denim trousers and a round-necked, well-fitting, soft green sweater. She had also washed her hair and brushed it out carefully once it was dry and tied it back with a green ribbon she had found among Serena's collection. And she'd liberally anointed herself with body lotion and found an old bottle of moisturiser which she had applied to her face. Other than that, it's the essential me, she had mused, eyeing herself in the mirror rather antagonistically. But she had been struck by that look of antagonism and pondered it, and warned herself not to allow it to flow over towards Grevil Robertson. Calm, definite and as gracious as possible is how I will be this morning. Won't I?

'Grevil, then,' she said to him with a brief smile, but knowing full well that she would, from now on, studiously avoid calling him anything. 'I . . . '

'This is excellent coffee, Kate. Why don't you sit down and join me?'

She realise she was still holding the coffee pot aloft although she'd poured her own. She put it down and sat down opposite him. He smiled at her and she could actually feel her hackles rising. He's making me feel like a guest in my own home, she thought. How does he do it?

'I don't know how to thank you Mr . . . er . . . and I truly appreciate your offer . . . '

'Grevil,' he supplied.

'*Yes,*' she said through her teeth, then she forced herself to smile although her grey eyes had flashed with anger. 'I truly appreciate your offer, but I can't . . . '

'I've had a better idea,' he interrupted, sitting back and stretching out his long legs.

'About what?'

He grinned. '*You.* Um . . . last night when I got back to Eton I went to see my manager, Stan Ellis. He's been here for over a year now and he knows the area pretty thoroughly. And according to him, Kunnunurra's most valuable assets are the three hundred acres of river flats on the other side of the creek.' He looked down at her enquiringly.

'Well, yes,' she said. 'I have two reasonable paddocks on this side of the creek but then the ground rises and it's more suitable for winter grazing.'

'That's what Stan said. Had you ever thought of leasing those three hundred acres out?'

She stared at him dazedly. 'Not really. I mean, I'd have to find someone to lease them to and . . . ' She stopped. 'Are you . . . ?' She stopped again.

'Yes. I'd be very interested in leasing them from you. And before you start on about charity again, Mrs Wiley,'—his hazel eyes glinted—'may I point out that I would make more money from the deal than you would, although along with the lease payments I'd be prepared to pay you a percentage of the profit I made on the crops grown there.'

Kate's mouth dropped open and when she shut it finally she tried to speak but found she couldn't.

'It makes good business sense from both our points of view, Kate,' he said at last, rather gently. 'I have direct access through our mutual boundary, it's prime land, and, while it won't net *you* what it would have otherwise, it will still bring you an income, but free you of some immediate burdens. All the costs, seed, fertiliser, aerial spraying, harvesting, etc, will be borne by Eton. Moreover, because it will be part of a much bigger operation, our costs will be much less than you could do it for.'

Kate took several deep breaths then stood up abruptly and walked over to the window.

And unbeknown to her, Grevil Robertson studied the line of her slender shoulders and slim back rather acutely.

She turned to him at last and her grey eyes were misty but she wasn't crying. 'I don't know what to say.' Her voice was husky.

'Just say yes, Kate.'

'I . . . Do you always get your own way?' She bit her lip. 'I didn't mean it to sound like that. Sorry. I guess I'm a bit flummoxed. I was quite determined to . . . ' She looked at him helplessly.

'Knock me back?' he asked softly.

'Yes . . . No . . . Well . . . '

'Do you think I don't know that?' He looked amused. 'You could always tell yourself you're doing it for Matt's and Serena's sake, you know.'

She flushed and he watched and waited with one eyebrow raised quizzically.

'No,' she said at last, very quietly. 'For my own sake it's like a miracle and I—I accept. Thank you. I really don't know how to thank you because I know it still goes back to Mike and what he did but . . . '

He cut her off with a wry look and she winced inwardly, thinking she was making a mess of being grateful. Will I *ever* learn how to be gracious? But then I *do* know he wouldn't be doing this otherwise and the talk of all the profit in the world can't change that!

She tilted her chin defiantly at him and opened her mouth to speak further on the subject but he laughed and stood up and said, 'That's better. I prefer you not trying to be grateful, Kate. I'm going into Toowoomba now and I'll see my solicitor and have him draw up the lease agreements. He'll post them out to you to get your signature. We might as well do things legally and shipshape, don't you agree? By the way, Tom would like Matt and Serena to come over to Eton one afternoon. How about Wednesday? I'll drop them home.'

That afternoon, Kate got a phone call from the solicitor, who turned out to be her solicitor as well—he had handled Mike's estate and had known her father—and he said that, having her interests at heart as well, he had thought he would advise her that the contracts he was drawing up were sound and beneficial to those interests.

Kate chatted to him for some time and he told her the figures Grevil Robertson had suggested: the quarterly lump sum lease payments and the percentage of profits.

Later, at the kitchen table, she did some cautious arithmetic and stared down at the results with dazed eyes. Because apart from the payments she would receive, her grain cheque was looking considerably more substantial now that she wouldn't have to spend any part of it on making the river flats productive—and her whole future on Kunnunurra had depended on that. Then, in the future, there was the percentage of profits to look forward to.

'Glory Hallelujah,' she said wryly as she nibbled the end of her pen. 'Did I say something about miracles to Marcie yesterday? This means,'—she glanced at the figures again—'I'll have no mortgage repayment worries, I'll be able to put in a crop on my side of the creek, I'll be able to hire some casual labour to help with all the repairs, I'll be able to refurbish all our wardrobes—and I'll even be able to afford a new washing machine!'

She stared out of the window and found herself wondering why she didn't feel more elated. Because of him? She pondered. A bit, perhaps, but not altogether . . .

Two days later, Marcie Hunter said to Kate, 'There! Now you can't say a word to me about sticking my oar in it. And you can't hate the man now, surely!'

'Naturally not,' Kate said.

Marcie narrowed her sparkling green eyes but with rare tact didn't pursue the matter. 'Well, tell me what your plans are?' she demanded enthusiastically instead.

Kate started to tell her but was interrupted after a very little while.

'Forget about this paddock or what you're going to do with that one!' Marcie said imperiously. 'It's you personally I'm interested in. God knows, you've subjugated yourself to this place long enough.'

'Well, I did think,' Kate said doubtfully, 'of trying to make myself over—a new woman, if you know what I mean. The only thing is, I don't quite know where to start.' She shrugged.

'Oh, Kate,' Marcie said softly and lovingly, but it had a strange effect on Kate. She stared at Marcie, blinked once then laid her head on the table and burst into tears.

It was a protracted bout of weeping, intense and painful, and nothing Marcie said helped so she stopped talking and just stroked Kate's hair gently.

'What I mean is,' Kate wept finally, 'there doesn't seem to be any point. Who cares? *I* don't seem to any more. I don't even seem to care that Kunnunurra's been saved . . . '

'Kate, look, love,' Marcie said softly, 'this is reaction. You've been strong for so long, under so much strain, it's a miracle you didn't have some kind of a breakdown ages ago.'

'Then why am I having one now? When there's no need!'

'That's the way it often happens, believe me. What you really need is a holiday.'

'When you've got stock you can't just walk away from the place, Marcie!'

'All right, all right.' Marcie stared down at Kate's bowed head thoughtfully. 'Look, I've got an idea. It's school holidays in a week's time and Rob's going down to Brisbane for an education seminar for the first week. I thought of going too, with Pete, but we went to one a couple of years ago and I was bored stiff. So, what say we come and stay with you? The kids would enjoy it, we could give them some special treats, take them into town—there should be a circus somewhere, that kind of thing—we could go shopping . . . '

Kate lifted her head at last. 'Do you . . . Would you . . . ' she said huskily.

'I can assure you I'd like nothing better,' Marcie said. Then her eyes twinkled. 'On one condition— no talk about paddocks and planting and all that nonsense.'

'It's not . . . I promise!' Kate said with a watery smile.

CHAPTER THREE

THERE was only one occasion during the first week of the school holidays that Kate had cause to break her promise.

'I'm sorry,' she said to Marcie, 'but I'll have to round up my cattle this afternoon. They're being picked up tomorrow; I'm sending them to the sales.'

Marcie cocked an eyebrow. 'Can we help?'

Kate hesitated. Matt and Pete had gone to cubs and, whereas Matt might have been some help, Serena was frightened of the cattle and Marcie, she knew, inexperienced, although game for anything.

'Er . . . ' she temporised.

Marcie laughed. 'It's all right, I get the picture. You'd rather do it alone. And in the meantime Serena and I will try out this recipe for a walnut cake, won't we, pet?'

Serena agreed happily.

Thank God for Marcie, Kate thought as she whistled for Digby and climbed into the ute. In only five days she's somehow made life worth living again. Mind you, we've packed so much into five days—two movies, dinner and shopping in Toowoomba, the circus at Dalby, a new wardrobe with her help—a bonfire of my old things! And I've been pampered and fussed over and, with Serena's connivance, massaged and manicured, and strange concoctions put in my hair, not to mention having had it fashionably cut, and been put on a fortifying and beautifying diet . . .

'Except for being on the thin side, your figure doesn't need much doing to it,' Marcie had said. 'When one gets down to it, it's really classy—perhaps there's something to be said for manual labour after all. But why do you hide it?

'I don't—do I?'

'Well anyway, no more baggy, shapeless clothes! I'm quite sure it's possible to be a lady farmer and well dressed at the same time. Especially when you have the figure for it.'

'Then why am I drinking carrot juice and forti-fied milk and so on?' Kate had enquired.

'Two reasons. You need a few more pounds on you, just a few, and it's not only what you put *on* your hair and skin that counts, it's what you put inside, too. You wait and see!'

' . . . And *you* wait and see, you baldy faces,' Kate said out of the ute window as she drove down the track and gazed around for her cattle. 'You just don't know what's about to hit you! A well-dressed lady farmer.'

It had seemed like sacrilege to wear what she was wearing to round up cattle. But when she had mentioned this to Marcie earlier, she'd been firmly taken to task.

'What's so special about ordinary jeans anyway?' Marcie had concluded.

'Ordinary! They cost a small fortune.'

'That's because they're well cut and well made and will last.'

'What if I tear them?'

'They'll still be well cut with a patch on them.'

'I'd kill myself if I tore this jacket,' Kate had said of her new quilted anorak in a soft sage green.

'Darling Kate,' Marcie had said patiently, 'these are your working clothes. They're smart but durable and they're by no means all you possess. *Will* you go down now and round up your cattle and stop quibbling!'

Kate had gone, but not before she'd heard Serena say, 'It's a good thing you burnt most of the others, Marcie.'

She grinned as she brought the truck to a halt. 'But one thing they didn't burn,' she said to Digby as she got out, 'is my old hat. Without which, in this type of operation, I'd be lost. But the only reason they didn't burn it is because I hid it!' She looked affectionately at the disreputable, wide-brimmed khaki hat and then set it jauntily on her head. 'Right, to work, old man,' she said to the dog. 'You take the flank, I'll take the rear and don't you take any cheek from these old cows!'

There was an art to rounding up cattle. Kate had realised this years ago and worked to perfect herself at it. Because one person who knew what they were doing was worth six who didn't, however enthusiastic they were.

The main thing was to be calm and deliberate and quite sure of yourself, and to wave your hat gently, and there was a special whistle you employed.

Her twelve steers were enjoying an afternoon siesta when she and Digby approached and they turned their heads lazily before scrambling up rather petulantly.

'Come on, you lazy things,' she sang out as they stood in a bunch and watched her approach. 'Don't just stand there!' She whistled and flicked her hat and Digby barked shrilly.

Eleven of them turned and begun to plod away. One stood his ground with his great white curly head lowered, his pink-rimmed, reddish brown eyes bulging. 'Sool him, Digby!' Kate commanded.

The dog darted in between the steer's legs and out like a flash of greased lightening. The steer snorted, turned on all fours like a ballerina, kicked his back legs skittishly, and trotted off to join his companions.

From then on it was plain sailing until they reached the gate of the holding pen. In fact, Kate discovered she was enjoying herself. It was a beautiful day for once, cold but very clear with the sky a wide dome of cloudless blue and the dry grass looking golden in the winter sunshine.

They put up a hare that bounded away towards the rockier ground that was a perfect camouflage for its dun, streaky fur. Digby nobly ignored it and concentrated on the task to hand.

The fact that Kate had the creek on her left helped considerably, but, as usual, while she could have gone on droving them all day, getting them to enter the holding pen was not quite so simple. The trick normally was to concentrate on one because, if you managed to manoeuvre one in, the rest generally followed.

Today she got eleven in, but the same one that had put up a show of boldness earlier refused steadfastly to go in and worse, enticed the others out.

'You stupid great beast!' Kate yelled, then took a deep breath. 'OK, Digby, let's try again. J-u-s-t slowly . . . Hang on!' She looked around, real-

ising she had made a tactical error. She had brought
feed down in the back of the ute for the night they
were to spend in the pen and she should have put it
in the pen to start with. But it was a fair walk back
to the ute now and in the process they could all
come back with her. 'Damn!' she muttered. 'I'm
losing my touch. I must have been day-dreaming!
I'll give it one more go.'

The same thing happened. Eleven steers went in,
which was something of a miracle because they were
getting stirred up, but the same one displayed the
same reluctance.

Kate swore inwardly but went on whistling and
patiently moving around it. Then the unexpected
happened: the steer turned actively aggressive. It
lowered its head and, with a loud bellow, charged
her.

But it had happened to her before and she took
evasive action smartly and that was when she came
to grief. She caught the heel of her boot on a stone
and tripped.

The next few moments were the most terrifying
of her life. She started to fall and could visualise
herself being trampled to death when a strong pair
of arms materialised out of nowhere and scooped
her out of the way in the nick of time.

She was then deposited on her feet with a
muttered, 'Stay where you are!' And had the
doubtful felicity of seeing Grevil Robertson round
up her recalcitrant steer as if it was no more
dangerous than a pussy cat—indeed, it trotted into
the pen like a lamb.

'Of all the . . . !' she exclaimed furiously, but
delayed reaction took over. She swayed as he

walked back towards her and would have fallen if
he hadn't put an arm round her shoulders. He said,
'Are you all right, Kate?'

'I . . . ' Kate found herself leaning against the
tall, strong length of him and for a moment forgot
what she'd been going to say—rather, found her
mind curiously blank.

Then an odd kind of agitation overcame her and
she pulled away saying brightly, 'I'm fine, thanks!
But . . . I'll just sit down for moment if you don't
mind.' And she did just that, rather abruptly, in the
dust.

'Sure?' he queried.

She looked up after a long hesitation. Apart from
when he had dropped Matt and Serena home the
week before, it was the first time she'd seen him since
the morning he had suggested the leasing arrangement. He hadn't stopped to talk the evening he had
dropped the children off. But she had signed the
lease documents and already received her first
payment. She had rung Eton up with the intention
of thanking him, but had got his manager and the
news that he would be away out west for a few days.
There had been no activity on the leased paddocks
as yet, but a gate had been put through the fence
she'd so laboriously repaired.

'I'm all right. Well, a little shaken up,' she
confessed. 'How did *you* get here?' But as soon as
the words had been uttered she winced inwardly
and thought how typically ungracious they had
sounded.

It seemed Grevil Robertson was not in the mood
to take offence, however, which galled Kate further,
although she couldn't say why.

He grinned down at her and said mildly, 'I was over the other side of the creek, pottering about on my horse, when I saw you working your steers. So I came over to see if I could help.'

Kate looked around and for the first time noticed a saddle horse cropping the grass a few feet away.

She switched her gaze away to inspect her boots rather darkly. Then she sighed and looked up again and said wryly, 'Thank you for saving my life. I'm usually better than that. You seem to . . . ' Make a habit of saving me, she had been going to say, but changed it to, 'seem to have the misfortune to always catch me on my bad days.'

Grevil Robertson raised a hand to push his hair off his forehead and replied gravely, 'I quite understand how you feel. There's nothing more infuriating, is there?'

Even seated more or less at his feet, Kate could see the amusement in his hazel eyes and the thought ran through her mind that she was just no match for this man. And what was more, just the sight of him, standing over her in his well-fitting khaki twill trousers that were tucked neatly into his elastic-sided boots, and in a bulky grey sweater with military patches on it, filled her with a very strange sort of apprehension.

But she couldn't sit there all day and be laughed at, she decided, and tried to scramble up, only to have him help her politely.

'Thanks,' she said breathlessly. 'If I've done anything to my clothes that will be the last straw,' she added, only for something to say, she realised, as she twisted her head to inspect her rear.

'There doesn't seem to be any damage,' Grevil Robertson murmured, and gave her a helping hand to brush herself down. 'New?' he asked as she stepped away.

'Yes.'

'They're very nice. Green suits you.'

Kate stared at him and thought suddenly that she must be going mad, because she would have given anything at that moment not to be wearing new clothes brought with *his* money Aha! That was the crunch bit, she decided—his money. It makes me feel like a charitable institution and I bitterly resent him complimenting me when he knows damn well I wouldn't be in new clothes if it wasn't for him. I am going mad, she mused, and managed to smile faintly and mutter, 'Thank you. Well, I suppose you'll be wanting to get back. And so should I. I've got visitors staying.'

'I'll walk back to your ute with you,' he said easily, and whistled for the horse which trotted up obediently. 'As a matter of fact,'—he pulled the reins over its head—'I wanted to see you anyway.'

'Oh, I did try to get in touch with you,' Kate broke in. 'Um, everything is . . . I mean, thank you . . . '

'Good,' he said as she floundered. 'But that wasn't what I wanted to see you about.'

'It wasn't?'

'No. It was to deliver an invitation.'

'An . . . Oh!' Kate said, taken completely by surprise.

'Yes. My grandmother has expressed a desire to meet you.'

Kate looked astonished. 'Me?'

'Yes, you,' Grevil Robertson said idly. 'She was much impressed with Serena and Matt the other day.'

'They—they mentioned her,' Kate said bemusedly. 'I did wonder if they'd got it wrong—about her being Tom's great-grandmother, I mean. She doesn't sound terribly old.'

'She's in her late seventies but she's amazingly spry. She was a very young bride and mother. Which, she claims, is what should happen to all girls—gets the silliness out of them, she thinks.'

Kate blinked then laughed. 'And what do you think?' she asked finally.

He considered her with the utmost gravity. 'I don't think I should venture an opinion.'

'Why not?'

'I've a feeling you might have equally strong views on the subject and I shouldn't like to offend you. Anyway, as a mere male . . . '

'Oh, bosh!' Kate said

'You don't have strong views on the subject of women's liberation?'

'Yes, I do—some, at least, but . . . How did we get on to this?'

'My grandmother started it, I believe . . . '

'And that's the other thing,' Kate said forcefully. 'I don't understand why she should want to meet me. Unless—did you tell her all about me?'

'Why not?'

'I don't . . . '

'I also told her about Mike. Unlike some people, the thought of my life being saved appealed to her,' he said a little drily, but went on lightly, 'And of course Tom is so full of his new friends. Will you come?'

They had reached the ute and stopped walking and he looked at her very directly.

'I . . . ' Kate hesitated.

'To afternoon tea next Tuesday? I must warn you she's a bit eccentric but lovable for all that. At least I find her so. She's also a bit lonely at the moment.'

'I . . . All right,' Kate said slowly.

'And bring the kids, naturally. Tom tells me Serena has quite reversed her original opinion of him.' Something in those hazel eyes glinted.

Unlike her mother's of Tom's father? Is that what you're saying? Kate thought, but did not ask. She said instead, 'I believe she has. Thank you. What time?'

'Three-thirty for four. She'll be looking forward to it, Mrs Wiley,' Grevil Robertson said straight-facedly but with a wicked glint of laughter in his eyes now. 'No,' he added softly, as Kate opened her mouth, 'you don't have to return the compliment. The last thing I'd like to be responsible for is you telling polite lies. All the same, I'll be surprised if you don't like my grandmother. In fact I think you and she might be two of a kind in some ways. See you later!' He mounted his patient horse with a flourish and rode away with a wave, leaving Kate staring after him with tight lips.

'I don't care what you say,'—Marcie looked pecul-iarly obstinate—'and I *knew* you still didn't like the man, despite your protests to the contrary . . . '

'I never said I liked him,' Kate interrupted. It was late that evening and they were sharing a nightcap in front of the fire. 'I merely said that I no longer hated him, or something to that effect.'

'Don't split hairs, Kate,' Marcie said sternly. 'The fact is, you've taken an unreasonable dislike to a perfectly charming, not to mention wildly attractive man who, on top of all that,' she paused dramatically, 'has helped you out of a very real crisis!'

Kate stared into the fire and watched little tendrils of bark catch alight, curl up and die. 'Perhaps that's it,' she said with a shrug. 'I do dislike having to be grateful to people. It seems to bring out the worst in me.' She looked at Marcie wryly, and narrowed her eyes. 'Have you met him then?'

'What makes you say that?' Marcie asked innocently.

'You were singing his praises with a degree of enthusiasm that didn't sound as if it was acquired second hand.'

'It was not.' Marcie grinned impishly. 'I met him on the last day of school. He came to see Roy about Tom—whether changing schools mid-year was causing him any problems. I thought he was gorgeous!'

'I'm shocked, Marcie,' Kate said with mock severity.

'I know. I know! But being married and a mother doesn't automatically mean your powers of aesthetic appreciation go on the blink.' Her green eyes sparkled wickedly and Kate had to laugh. She also happened to know that Marcie was very much in love with her quiet, scholarly husband.

'But to get back to what I was saying.' Marcie looked determined again. 'To knock back an invitation to meet his grandmother is crazy! Apart from anything else, you do realise that most people for miles around would give their eye teeth to be invited to Eton?'

'I'm not knocking it back—I can't now without making a fool of myself,' Kate said irritably. 'But that doesn't mean to say I'm jumping for joy about it.'

'What have you got against his grandmother?'

'I've got nothing against his grandmother. How could I? I don't even know her.'

'Precisely. So what have you got against him that automatically turns you off his grandmother who you don't even know?' Marcie demanded.

'Marcie!' Kate said exasperatedly. 'Will you stop trying to tie me up in knots . . . ' She broke off, realising suddenly how angry she'd sounded. 'Sorry,' she said ruefully and even laughed at herself.

Marcie laughed, too, but then she said, 'Seriously, Kate, what is it?'

'Seriously?' Kate pondered a moment. 'I don't know.'

'You don't think,' Marcie said softly, 'you might have imagined that . . . Well, you said the reason you found him hateful was . . . ' She hesitated and looked uncomfortable. 'What I mean is, he didn't look to me the kind of man who gets around like King Solomon—as you put it. You don't think you imagined it, do you? You were very upset about the washing machine, remember?'

Kate grinned suddenly. 'I didn't imagine it,' she said, 'and thank you for reminding me of it, because it gives me something solid to base my 'irrational'—as *you* put it—dislike of the man on.'

'But . . .'

'Darling,' Kate said gently, 'I'm not going to like Grevil Robertson and that's that. Oh, I'll be suitable grateful and I'll try not to show it and I'll go and see his grandmother—I'll be the perfect charitable institution, so don't worry, but like him, no.'

'Kate,' Marcie said abruptly, 'don't you think you're playing with fire?'

Kate blinked. 'I don't know what you mean,' she said, and didn't. 'He won't back out, it's too late.' She bit her lip and looked faintly embarrassed.

'That's not what I meant.'

'What did you mean then?' Kate asked.

'I—don't really know. Just a funny feeling,' Marcie said slowly.

Some time later, Kate turned over restlessly in bed because, despite her show of bravado to Marcie, she was again in the grip of that strange, nameless apprehension that even thinking of Grevil Robertson seemed capable of engendering—when she wasn't feeling angry with him, that was.

How I wish to God I'd never laid eyes on him, she mused, and punched her pillow rather viciously.

Tuesday came around far too quickly for Kate's liking. Marcie and Pete had gone home and it was another clear sunny day, which also annoyed her. She had been hoping for floods.

When they were dressed and ready to go, her nerves manifested themselves in a ferocious attack with the broomstick on Billy the goat, caught nibbling at the washing on the line. 'That's it!' she said, breathing heavily and resting on the broom. 'If he won't learn, he goes!'

'Mum, you might have hurt him,' Serena said reproachfully.

Kate snorted. 'He's got a hide like a rhinoceros—that's the problem! If I ever did manage to give him one good hiding he might not be so naughty. But from now on he stays outside the garden. Right?'

'He'll be terribly lonely then,' Matt objected. 'Digby's his friend.'

'Well that might teach him.' Kate cast the broom away and looked her offspring over critically then marched them inside to brush their hair again to the tune of their chorused disapproval. 'We've just brushed it, Mum!'

'Once more won't hurt. There. Now go and sit in the ute; I'll be with you in a moment. And don't you dare get dirty!'

Serena rolled her eyes expressively but grabbed Matt's sleeve and pulled him outside.

'What's wrong with Mum?' Kate heard Matt say as they passed the bedroom window.

'She's worried about going to Eton,' his twin sister replied.

'Why?'

' 'Cause, silly, it's the first time for her and it's a big honour and . . . '

Kate rolled her own eyes as they moved out of earshot, then she found himself smiling rather shame-facedly at herself in the mirror. 'Count to ten, Kate Wiley,' she murmured ruefully.

She picked up her own brush and fiddled with it and examined herself critically. The skirt she wore had been Marcie's choice; pale grey wool and gored, it fitted around her hips perfectly. The buttercup angora sweater she wore had been her own choice, as had the grey suede shoes with medium heels.

But it was almost like looking at a stranger, a tall willowy stranger, or someone from the past. It's funny, she reflected, I actually feel taller, and I can't have grown so it must have been a mental shrinking, an inner disgust that I was looking such a mess. And I think Marcie was right about her inner cosmetics; my skin feels softer and smoother and my hair is starting to shine again.

She put up a hand to touch her thick chestnut hair that fell to just above her shoulders now, then grimaced because her hands still gave the game away.

The horn of the ute beeped twice, cheekily, and Kate sighed, took a deep breath and picked up her bag.

It was Grevil Robertson's grandmother who came out to greet them on the wide, pillared veranda of Eton homestead. She was a tall, striking old lady, beautifully dressed in a matching fuchsia pink tweed skirt and twinset, and she had Grevil's hazel eyes and a magnificent head of very white hair worn on top of her head in a bun.

She said immediately, 'You must be Kate Wiley but I shall call you Katherine. I deplore the shortening of names and I don't know why you allow it. Katherine is much prettier than plain Kate, surely?'

'Er . . . ' Kate detected from the twins' expressions of muffled mirth that they had already been subjected to this, but Mrs Robertson went on without waiting for a reply, 'I'm delighted to see you though, Katherine! And there you are, Matthew and Serena. Now would you believe Thomas has been getting around like a cat on hot bricks for hours, but now he's disappeared . . . '

'No, I haven't, I'm here, Gran!' Tom erupted on to the veranda with his usual wide grin and bore Matt and Serena off with him.

'Your tea will be in the kitchen!' Mrs Robertson called after them and turned back to Kate. 'You have charming children, Katherine. Do come inside!'

Kate followed her into a beautifully appointed room which, she thought immediately, could only be described as a drawing-room. But before she was asked to sit down, Mrs Robertson stood in front of her and examined her candidly from head to toe until an uncomfortable tide of colour rose in her cheeks. She could think of absolutely nothing to say, either.

'Well,' Grevil's grandmother said at last with a twinkle in her eyes, 'I like what I see, Katherine. Good bones, perhaps a trifle on the thin side—men don't really go for that, you know—and your hands are in a bad way,'—Kate repressed a desire to hide her hands behind her back—'but yes, a womanly woman, I would say, and at the same time a capable one. I admire that. I do hope you're not a radical feminist, Katherine. I don't admire that. I think it is very important to be able to get on with men, don't you? Not to be subservient but to have an understanding of them, because once you understand them they became so much easier to handle. Do sit down, my dear.'

Kate sat a little dazedly and prayed she wouldn't be expected to reply in kind. Mrs Robertson sat down opposite her, crossed her still slender ankles elegantly and chuckled.

'Don't mind me, my dear,' she said warmly. 'I'm renowned for speaking my mind. Do you know, I got quite a different impression of you from what Grevil said.'

I can imagine, Kate thought acidly, but she murmured, 'I'm not surprised really. I was in a bad way the first time we met.'

'Tell me all about it!' Mrs Robertson commanded with relish.

And to her astonishment, Kate found herself doing just that, although she omitted the exact nature of the look Grevil Robertson had first given her. She found his grandmother unusually understanding.

'I can just imagine it,' Mrs Robertson said wryly. 'I've told Grevil that he sometimes gets around as lord and master of all he surveys but I'm afraid it's an inherited characteristic. My son and my husband were the same. Very irritating it is, though, and I'm thrilled that you actually slammed the door on him! How brave of you.'

Kate grimaced and coloured. 'I'm not thrilled, really,' she admitted.

'Now what's done is done, so it's no good having regrets,' Mrs Robertson said firmly. 'Tell me about your husband, Katherine. I believe we Robertsons are rather indebted to him!'

'Well . . . ' Kate hesitated.

But by the time they had had a traditional tea with two kinds of cake, cucumber sandwiches and tiny hot scones, served on a magnificent Spode tea service, she had, in fact, told Mrs Robertson most of her life story.

'I think you had a very sound upbringing,' the old lady said approvingly. 'I'd be interested to see your collection of china one day and, before you go, remind me to take you into the dining-room to see the rest of ours. Although is isn't all quite unpacked yet. I like to do things slowly, Katherine. Even moving and unpacking. Take your time is one of my mottoes.'

'Do you like the Darling Downs, Mrs Robertson?' Kate asked. 'It must be rather a change for you.'

'Well, I'm used to that. After Grevil married I went away to live in Sydney—we've always maintained a house there—but when Solange died I went back to look after Thomas. He was very little, you see—so sad. But anyway, it is a change, Katherine, one I wouldn't have made myself because our principal property out west was my home for so long. But it is very isolated and, apart from that, I can understand that Grevil wanted to make a fresh start. You haven't thought of doing that, by the way?'

'Doing . . . ?'

'Well, it is four years since your Mike died, you told me. And from what I gather, since then it's been all hard work. And there have been no men in your life?'

'No.'

'Perfectly natural,' Mrs Robertson said briskly, but added, 'up to a point.'

'I don't think I quite . . . '

'Oh, I'm not suggesting you should be a merry widow, but I think it's time you . . . '

'Mrs Robertson,' it was Kate's turn to interrupt, 'you're very kind to be concerned, but . . . '

'You don't think it's any of my business?'

'No,' Kate said.

'Excellent! Not many people can say no to me, Katherine, and I always admire the ones who do. But let me point our that I'm only speaking generally. I don't think it's wise or healthy for any woman to live like a nun,' she said vigorously. 'Now that's my opinion. Others will differ, but from your point of view and what you've told me of your life, I think the time has come to open it up, to get out and meet some men, to think of marrying again.'

Kate drew a breath, but a voice from behind said, 'Dear Gran, don't you think you should leave that to Kate to decide?'

'Why, Grevil,' Mrs Robinson said easily, 'I didn't hear you come in. Have you been home long? I was merely trying to give Katherine some advice.

Grevil Robertson strolled into Kate's view. It was obvious from his damp hair that he had been home long enough to shower and he was wearing perfectly pressed grey trousers and a mulberry sweater over a dazzlingly white shirt. And for the life of her, as he looked at her quizzically, Kate couldn't help herself from remembering, with a kind of deadly accuracy, the ease with which he had lifted her out of the path of her angry steer, the strength of his arms . . . Why *that?* she asked herself angrily.

'Embarrassing her, Gran, I would have said,' he remarked, and added, 'How are you today, Mrs Wiley?'

'Very well, thank you, Mr Robertson,' Kate replied after a moment.

'How formal we are!' Mrs Robertson marvelled. 'I thought you two knew each other better than that—now.' She cast Kate a mischievous look.

'Perhaps we need a glass of sherry to . . . wind us up,' Grevil Robertson said with an amused look Kate. 'It is that time, anyway.'

Kate glanced at her watch and started with surprise. 'I really ought to be getting home. I had no idea it was so late.'

'Nonsense! Give her a glass, Grevil,' Mrs Robertson commanded. 'And by the way, I'm sure I was not embarrassing Katherine earlier. She's not a silly young girl, are you, my dear?'

'I hope not.' Kate accepted her glass of sherry with a swift upward look and could have kicked herself for not having had the sense to leave earlier. For those hazel eyes were still laughing at her.

'Besides,' Mrs Robertson went on, 'I was only giving her the same advice I gave you, Grevil. Which you saw fit to follow, I'm happy to say.'

'Which advice was that? You've given me so much over the years I get confused,' her grandson said wryly. He hadn't sat down after pouring the sherry from the crystal decanter set on a lovely, mahogany, Sheraton-style drum table with curved legs and an inlaid top, but was leaning against the elegant marble mantelpiece.

'Don't be obtuse, Grevil,' the old lady reproved, 'you were obviously eavedropping. The advice to remarry, of course!' She turned to Kate. 'Grevil had a similar experience to you, Katherine. He lost a beloved wife—a lovely girl she was, too. It was very sad. But time does heal if you'll let it and now Grevil is engaged to another lovely girl—you'll meet her soon. Unfortunately her father was taken gravely ill recently, otherwise she'd be here now, wouldn't she, Grevil?'

Grevil Robertson had not lifted his gaze from its contemplation of his sherry glass while his grandmother spoke, but he did now, abruptly. And he caught Kate looking at him open-mouthed.

They stared at each other then he smiled slightly and said, 'That surprises you. Perhaps you thought I was too big-headed to appeal to anyone as a marriage proposition?'

'I . . . No!' Kate stammered, at the same time wondering a little wildly why she felt as if she'd received a blow to the solar plexus. 'No, I'm very happy for you!' she managed to add.

'Thank you,' he said with irony. 'But I must point out that I wasn't consciously following my grandmother's famous advice. It was something that merely happened,'

'Oh, now, do give me some credit . . . '

Kate stayed for another ten minutes, listening to their light-hearted banter but thinking some rather strange thoughts. Then she put her empty glass down and stood up and made her excuses as firmly but as graciously as she could.

'I've really enjoyed meeting you, Mrs Robertson,' she said on the front veranda, and found she meant it.

'So have I, my dear Katherine,' Mrs Robertson replied and kissed her on the cheek. 'You must come again. Oh, we didn't get a chance to see the china! Well, now there's no excuse for you not to come. I'm afraid I'm not going to stay out here in the cold but Grevil will see you to your car. Goodbye, children!'

She kissed them, too and Grevil Robertson said to Kate as they walked down the front steps, 'You seem to have made a big hit, Mrs Wiley. I told you you would like her, didn't I?'

Kate glanced sideways and encountered that look of amusement she was coming to know so well. 'You not only get your own way but you're always right, aren't you?' she muttered before she could stop herself. Then a flood of irritation, or something, engulfed her and she added, 'I wish you'd make up your mind and call me one thing or the other!'

'I only call you Mrs Wiley on the occasions when I suspect I might get my face slapped for calling you anything else,' he murmured as they came up to the ute.

'Oh, bosh,' Kate said. 'As if I'd dream of slapping your face!'

'Not even dream of it?' he queried.

Kate opened her mouth but, as he laughed softly, she coloured and closed it, and closed her eyes briefly in exasperation, only to open them and rather sharply command Matt and Serena to get in.

They complied with slightly started looks but Tom, apparently oblivious to the nuances, raced round to the other side so he could talk to them through the window. Just as Kate was about to slide in herself, Grevil Robertson put a hand on her arm and somehow or other contrived to close the door and turn her away from it.

'What do you think you're doing?' she demanded, but in an undertone.

'I thought we once agreed that we don't take your differences out on eight-year-olds,' he said, also in an undertone, but a surprisingly grim one.

'They're not *my* . . . ' Kate caught her breath and forced herself to think before she spoke. 'I'm sorry.' she said with an effort. 'You're right.'

'Am I?' he countered. 'Well then, why don't you explain something else to me? What differences do we have?'

'I . . . ' Kate bit her lip and tried to free her arm as Matt and Serena, obviously sensing a delay, slipped out of the other door. 'Oh . . . '

'Let them go,' Grevil Robertson said in a hard voice.

'No.'

'Yes. And start talking, Kate. I'm waiting.'

'I . . . there's nothing to say. I like . . . ' She stopped helplessly.

'Go on. You like my son? My grandmother? I saw that. But not myself. I see that every time you look at me. And I can't help finding it a little strange.'

'I don't . . . I . . . ' Kate swallowed and looked away from those ironical hazel eyes. She tried again. 'I'm sorry if I've given you that impression because I'm very much in your debt.'

He said something Kate wouldn't have liked the children to hear, but even on her own account it reactivated her ever present surge of antagonism. 'There's no need to swear,' she said coldly. And because Grevil Robertson confused her and bothered her and definitely brought out the worst in her, she found herself going on, 'Look, I've told you how grateful I am to you, I've come to see your grandmother and told her, but I'm just not going to grovel to you!'

'Who said anything about grovelling? You're the one who's playing up this gratitude bit out of all proportion. I've told you before, there's no damned charity involved.'

Kate's breasts heaved. 'The point is,' she said through her teeth 'you don't need to make money out of my river flats and you wouldn't be doing it if it wasn't for Mike. Well, I'm grateful for that but I'd rather we kept it on a business footing. Why is it so important for me to like you anyway?'

A strange glitter came to Grevil Robertson's eyes as he stared down at her and Kate saw it. She trembled inwardly suddenly, and could have cut off her tongue because she knew she was being unreasonable and carrying this thing to ridiculous lengths, but the presence of this man seemed to be a like a goad to her flesh. Only these sane, reasonable thoughts, the first she'd entertained for a few minutes, had come too late, she knew, and now she was going to pay.

'You know what you need, Kate, don't you?' Grevil Robertson said pleasantly, in spite of that glitter of anger in his eyes. 'You need a man.'

A burning tide of colour poured into her cheeks and for a moment she was so stunned, she couldn't move a muscle. And not only because he had said it, but because of a burgeoning, horrifying suspicion that the echo of his words left in her mind. But it couldn't be, could it? No. Then why . . . No. *No.*

She swallowed and tore her eyes from his, and squared her shoulders in an unconsciously gallant gesture. And from God knows where, she found the composure to say, 'So everyone keeps telling me!'

He raised his eyebrows. 'Everyone?'

Your grandmother, Marcie . . . Now you. I think I'll have to consider it. You can't all be wrong, can you?'

'Kate.'

She had stared down at her unhealed hands while she spoke but she looked up at last. 'Yes?'

He was about to speak but the kids chose that moment to rush up, fortuitously for Kate, and Serena said, 'I'm cold, Mum!'

'Hop in then, love. We're really going this time. Goodbye, Tom! Thank you for having us. Goodbye. I . . . ' She slid into the ute and started the motor. 'It's been lovely. Goodbye.' And she drove off with a wave.

CHAPTER FOUR

'Mrs Wiley.'

'Mr Watson,' Kate said the next morning. She'd discovered that one of her indicators on the ute wasn't working and was waiting at the local garage while a new bulb was installed. Les Watson had just alighted from his latest model Holden estate car and come into the garage, doffing his broad-brimmed hat.

He was a big man, in his middle forties, with an arrogant manner and very blue eyes. For some reason she had never really discovered, those blue eyes had always gone unusually hard and cold whenever they rested on her, and nothing had changed today, she saw in the neon light of the garage. She had asked Mike about it once and he had said laughingly that Les Watson always made him feel as if he'd crawled out from under a stone, too.

'But why?' she had demanded to know.

'Probably because we're newcomers,' he had said. 'The Watsons have been here for generations and they probably think they're the only kind who should be here.'

But Kate had pointed out that the Morcambes had also been in the area for generations, longer than the Watsons, but they were really very nice— if they happened to recognise you. Mike's reply had been that some people were simply ignorant and

narrow-minded and resented newcomers whether
they were farmers or factory workers or whatever.

And with that, Kate had had to be content.

It was perhaps unfortunate that on that particular morning, the first person she should lay eyes
on after the garage mechanic was Les Watson. She
returned that cold, hard, very blue glance with a
chilly look of her own, tilted her chin defiantly at
him and deliberately turned her back on him.

There was a moment's silence. Then he drawled.
'My word, Mrs Wiley, we are uppity this morning.'

She swung round with her grey eyes suddenly
blazing but he only laughed softly, replaced his hat
precisely and walked out on her.

I hate *men,* Kate muttered to herself, grinding her
teeth. All of them, and I shall probably bite the next
person who tells me I need one of them!

But that afternoon, while she was gardening with
almost ferocious zeal, she suddenly threw away her
trowel and buried her head in her hands. Admit it,
Kate, she told herself, kneeling on an old sack in
the damp, cool grass. You're in trouble. From the
moment Grevil said that, it all started to come clear
to you, didn't it? Why else would an ultra-chauvin-
istic utterance like that suddenly flash an image into
your mind of not only needing a man, but needing
Grevil Robertson—an image of yourself, lying in
his arms . . .   You've tried to block it out of your
mind all night and all day but it isn't going to work!

She sank back on to her heels and hugged herself
and bit her lip almost hard enough to draw blood.
What a fool I am, she marvelled, not to *know* there
was an attraction, to have to have it virtually spelt
out for me. Why else would I have taken *such*

exception to that look? Why else do I always feel at such a disadvantage with him, hate being indebted to him, feel so . . . apprehensive when he's around? Why else would it have come as a shock to hear that he's getting married? Oh, God . . .

She stared painfully over the garden and across the acres of sun-dappled paddocks and found her cheeks were wet with tears because, apart from anything else, this was the first time she'd thought of another man in that way since Mike had died. Mike, who had *loved* her so.

'But this can't possibly be the same thing,' she whispered, rocking backwards and forwards, still hugging herself. A physical attraction, perhaps—I don't suppose actually being able to visualise going to bed with a man could be called an aesthetic interest. And you'd be insane to lump it under the heading of wanting to show a superior male a thing or two, but might you be able to attribute it to four years of celibacy?

'I don't know if I believe in that.'

The thought, uttered aloud, startled her, but she found herself pursuing it with a sense of fatalism. Do you have to fall in love with someone to want to sleep with them? Or does the body, especially one that's known . . . love, take over? Oh, God, I hope so, because I can cope with that, I think. Because I do believe it can only be a passing thing, that. A purely physical attraction. I mean to say, there are times when I genuinely *don't* like the man. I wonder if he suspects?

This new thought left her feeling hot and cold and brought to mind that look again. What kind of a man is he really? she asked herself. Would he take advantage of knowing this has happened to me?

'But he's never going to know, is he?' she whispered. 'Not from me, whatever he might suspect. Oh, no. Because now you've worked it all out, you can handle it, can't you? Can't you?'

Two mornings later, she was put to the test—and would never have believed how she did handle it.

She saw the maroon Range Rover drive up; she saw Grevil Robertson step out, clad in waterproofs and wellingtons because it had rained all night and was still raining. She herself had been up since five and out in the bad weather, but she had come in two hours ago and had a warm shower and was now respectably dressed in cream trousers and a cinnamon pullover. It was also her baking day and the kitchen was warm and inviting and deliciously aromatic. She had only come into her bedroom, which looked out over the front garden, to find a magazine with a recipe for gingerbread she thought she might try.

But as soon as she saw him, striding across her lawn, she forgot about the gingerbread because all the doubts she had entertained over the past two days—such as wondering whether she had imagined being attracted to Grevil Robertson, whether the years of strain and worry hadn't after all been too much for her and affected her mind—were swept away.

Because her heartbeat seemed to have tripled, her mouth was suddenly dry but her palms damp, and her breathing was erratic. And, worst of all, she was glad, she was terrified, she was filled with a haunting sadness to see him.

She was also frozen to the spot for some moments, so that by the time she responded to his knock with her apron, which she'd removed, still held clutched in one hand, he had taken off his dripping outerwear and was standing on her porch mat in his socks.

She digested this—it was obvious he intended to come in—in silence and heard herself say, 'Oh. Hello! What a lousy day,' all without actually looking him in the eye.

But when he said, 'Hello, Kate,' some compelling power made her look straight into those hazel eyes and find them sober and unamused.

She swallowed, then remembered her plan of action—be as natural as you possibly can with him, no more anger or bitterness, just calm and collected . . .

'Come in,' she said and stood back and was gratified for a moment to see a flicker of surprise in his eyes. 'Have you come to see me about something?'

'Two things,' he said, stepping inside and causing her small hall to shrink. She closed the front door carefully and turned to find him standing in front of her.

'Well.' She half smiled and hoped to God she hadn't looked as nervous as she felt. 'I've—oh, actually I have just made a pot of tea. Would you like a cup? Just . . . I'm in the kitchen. I think you know the way.'

But it was his turn to stand aside to let her pass and she did. As she led the way she used every second of the short walk to try to compose herself.

'Sit down,' she said in the kitchen. 'I'm baking,' she added unnecessarily because the evidence of it was everywhere, even on the dining-table which she started to clear.

'It smells wonderful, but don't clear up on my account. You're obviously a lady of many talents, Kate,' he said, eyeing a plate of fresh, pricked, sugary shortbread.

'Not really,' she murmured. 'But we'll have some of that with our tea if you like.' She fetched the teapot from beside the stove, and cups and saucers, and wondered miserably what to say next. She also found herself trying to pinpoint what was different about his manner. His words seemed to indicate that he wasn't angry with her but there was a sort of reserve. Perhaps he thinks I'm still angry, she wondered. Little does he know—well, so I hope.

She poured milk and tea, passed him a cup and the sugar and the shortbread, all in silence.

'Has . . . '

'I came . . . '

Their words clashed.

'Go on.'

'No.' Kate said, 'it wasn't important. You go first. You came?' She looked at him with raised eyebrows.

'To see you about a drainage problem we have on the river flats. Have you been down that way today?'

'No! What's happened?' For the first time, even to her own ears, she sounded perfectly natural and she winced inwardly, especially as he smiled briefly.

'Well, about fifty acres are under water and from what I can see the problem seems to be some sort of obstruction in the creek, but further down.'

'The creek,' she said slowly, her attention now wholly caught. 'There's an old bridge, a very old wooden bridge that's too dangerous to use, further down. Parts of it are rotten. I wonder if it's collapsed? It was quite a solid bridge once—I mean there was a lot of timber used to build it. I've been meaning to do something about it for ages, but . . . ' She shrugged.

'That sounds as if it could be it. The water's obviously backing up and because the river flats are low . . . '

'Backing up?' she interrupted. 'H-how far?'

'Not past your river flats as yet,' he said.

'As yet,' she repeated hollowly and drank her tea in one swallow. 'Oh, hell!' She sprang up agitatedly. 'I'll have to do something right now.'

'Kate,' he said mildly 'there's no need to get into a sweat.'

'There's every need,' she contradicted him. 'I can just imagine how popular I'll be if it backs up any further and beyond my boundaries! It doesn't run through Eton, but that same creek runs through Les Watson's property and one in between and I happen to know Les has just sown a crop almost on its banks only a couple of miles upstream. If it got washed away because I was responsible for damming the creek, I'd never ever live it down. Do you mind——Would you mind very much . . . '

'Yes, I would,' Grevil Robertson said, and it popped into Kate's mind that *he* sounded more like his old self suddenly. And he was certainly eyeing her with amusement. 'Sit down,' he went on, 'and tell me what you intend to do.'

'Do?' She forgot all other thoughts and sat down, only to stand up restlessly again. 'Take the tractor down and see if I can clear it. I don't suppose this bloody rain will do me a favour and stop,' she said intensely. 'It never rains when I want it to so why should I expect the opposite?'

He grinned and looked at her quizzically and she had to stop pacing and smile back at him feebly. 'Don't mind me—I sometimes think I'm quite mad too,' she muttered. 'But, look, I do have to . . . '

'You're not serious—about trying to clear it yourself?' he said, suddenly quite serious himself.

'Yes, I am! I've got some chains on the tractor and tongs and . . . '

'You are mad, Kate Wiley!' he said standing up and taking her by the shoulders, catching her unawares. 'You could kill yourself out there on a tractor in these conditions alone, without trying to drag a bridge out of the creek.'

'But you don't understand! I have to try. What else is there to do? And there's a pretty good all-weather track from here down to the creek. Mike built it so we could get around in these conditions.'

'I don't care how many all-weather tracks you have,' he said roughly, 'you're only a woman!'

'But I . . . ' Tears of frustration shimmered in her eyes.

'Kate,' he said and swore beneath his breath, 'for another thing, why the hell do you think I'm here? I came to offer to help.'

'But it's not your responsibility. It's not part of the lease or . . . ' She stopped and bit her lip as his mouth hardened.

'You never give in, do you?' he said harshly. 'You know, I'm tempted to let you go down there and drown yourself because you're the most stubborn, unreasonable creature I've ever met!' His fingers bit into her shoulders as he gazed down at her furiously and contemptuously.

Kate winced and her mouth trembled and every good intention she'd ever had regarding this man rose up and taunted her—how she was going to handle him, how she was going to handle herself and this horribly ironic situation she'd got herself in to. But what had she done? Fallen straight into the same old trap. You *fool,* Kate! Perhaps it would be a good idea if you went out and drowned yourself. No . . .

She drew a shaky breath and sagged suddenly beneath his hands. 'I'm sorry,' she whispered. 'I don't know what gets into me sometimes. I think it's that I've been so used to doing everything on my own, I just don't stop to think. I . . . If you really wouldn't mind helping, I'd appreciate it.' She cleared her throat and strove for a lighter note. 'Les Watson and I . . . don't get on very well as it is, you see. I know he'll be absolutely furious. I guess that's why I panicked; he'd have good cause this time . . . ' She ran out of steam and stared up at Grevil Robertson wordlessly.

Gradually the pressure of his fingers lightened until he released her shoulders, but he put his hands back briefly to steady her, and said, with just a glimmer of a smile, 'What, may I enquire, have you done to antagonise this Les Watson?'

Some colour crept into Kate's cheeks but she knew she had deserved that and she managed to say ruefully, 'Strange to say, nothing. I know you might not believe that,' she smiled weakly, 'and you'd be entitled not to, but I think when he took his first look at me years ago, he decided he wasn't going to like me and he hasn't ever changed his mind. Well to be quite honest, lately I've . . . er . . . '

'Given him back as good as you got?' Grevil Robertson suggested.

'Something like that,' Kate confessed.

'I can imagine,' he murmured with a wry look.

'I don't think you can,' Kate replied with some spirit, but immediately looked a little shame-faced. 'The crazy part is it's a mostly unspoken thing,' she said perplexedly. 'Apart from what he says about me behind my back.'

'Oh? What things?'

Kate grimaced and began to wish she'd never enlarged on the sore subject of Les Watson. 'How I was ruining a good property and reduced to eating the flies off the wall,' she said hastily. Then she shrugged. 'But I guess it wasn't so far off the mark until you . . . I mean . . . came along. But let's not get into that. I mean . . . '

He was laughing outright now. 'No,' he said, 'let's not.' He touched her hot cheek with his fingers, just a fleeting, idle sort of salute, but her heart seemed to move in her breast, and he added, 'One thing about you, Mrs Wiley, you're never dull to be with. Well, shall we get this show on the road? Does any of your all-weather track extend to our mutual boundary? Because if so, I can ring Eton and bring in reinforcements and a more powerful tractor than yours, probably.'

'Yes. Yes,' she said, curiously husky, but he seemed not to notice and she went on to explain the track.

'Good,' he said and looked around for the phone.

'Are you going down, too?' she asked.

'Yes, I'll go down from this side.'

'Can . . . can I come? I won't interfere or anything like that.'

'Of course. I'll need you to navigate anyway.'

The bridge had indeed collapsed into the creek and, in the process, taken a large willow tree with it. Kate gasped when she saw how effectively the creek was being dammed and how much of her leased river flats were slowly disappearing under water.

'You haven't planted anything yet, have you?' she asked Grevil Robertson urgently.

'No. But we will be next week if the weather clears.'

'Thank God!'

She'd changed into jeans and a bright yellow mackintosh and hat, had the foresight to ring Marcie and ask her if she could keep Matt and Serena after school, and had climbed in beside Grevil Robertson for the slow, slippery trip down to the creek.

He said now, 'The rain must have weakened its foundations.'

They got out into the mud and drizzle. Fortunately, the creek wasn't very deep here, although Kate suspected that this had contributed to the old bridge's demise. It had never had much of a clearance and often went underwater. All the same, she knew she'd have had no chance of clearing it herself and was even doubtful that anyone else could until she saw the tractor from Eton trundling towards them. It was a late model, a lime green monster with an enclosed cabin, enormous wheels and, she had no doubt, refinements like a padded seat and roll bars, whereas her tractor was equipped with a cushion tied over the metal seat to protect her bottom and had no protection from the weather. With it came two men, one of whom was Stan Ellis, the Eton manager. Grevil introduced her to both of them and she was a little surprised at the deference they accorded her. She had thought they would be cursing her and her bridge.

Then she realised that, although they spoke together informally, there was some indefinable air about Grevil Robertson that proclaimed him the boss. And as she stood rather helplessly on the sidelines, listening to them working out a plan of action, she found herself adding that to her curiously precious store of knowledge about him—that he was a man among men.

Fortunately, again, the bridge itself had broken up considerably, but the tree had not and would have to be pulled out in one piece. They decided to do this first and Kate watched unhappily as Stan Ellis drove the tractor while Grevil and the other man waded waist-deep into the water to attach the chains. It was an unpleasant job at the best of times—both men had to hack through branches with axes—but in the rain and the cold and the mud . . .

Some of her unhappiness must have communicated itself because, finally, when the tree was clear of the creek, Grevil said to her with a grin, 'You

don't have to suffer every step of the way with us.
Why don't you get up with Stan? He can show his
new baby off to you.'

So she climbed gratefully up into the cabin of the
tractor and spent the next hour receiving instruc-
tions on how to drive it as load after load of wood
was attached and hauled clear.

Then it started to rain harder and Stan began to
look concerned. 'What we need is one more pair of
hands down there to get it cleared quicker. If this
keeps up we'll need flippers!' he shouted over the
rain.

Kate drew a quick little breath. 'I could handle
the tractor now. I—I've driven tractors for years
and never once rolled one. And from what you've
shown me . . . '

Stan looked at her shrewdly. 'I've seen you,' he
said. 'You're pretty damn good for a . . .   Pretty
good.' He hesitated then nodded decisively. 'All
right. I'll check it out with the boss. If he says yes,
OK. Just watch for signals.'

He climbed out and Kate saw him say something
to Grevil and spread his hands, then turn back to
her and give her a thumbs up sign.

Kate closed her eyes briefly then took her bottom
lip between her teeth and vowed she would go out
and shoot herself if she made one single slip.

She didn't. Finally it was done, the bed of the
creek was clear, the level of water had risen considerably and it was rushing downstream noisily. The
three men gave a ragged cheer and Kate got down
stiffly to join them. She found she wasn't too steady
on her legs as she tried to thank them and at the
same time apologise for rendering them soaked to

the skin, caked with mud and no doubt frozen, tired and sore.

'A pleasure, ma'am!' Grevil said, his teeth glinting white in a grin which didn't seem to be weary at all. 'You were rather good yourself.'

'Never thought it was possible!' the third man said admiringly. 'For a lady. My wife cain't get a car out of a parking lot without dinting it.'

Kate sniffed and blinked away a tear because they were being so nice; for some reason she was the one who was exhausted, although she'd done virtually nothing.

'Should all be down by morning,' Stan said. 'The water, I reckon. And if it isn't, it won't be your fault, Mrs Wiley. Just the jolly old rain!'

'It does rain rather a lot in these parts, I've noticed.'

Kate glanced across at Grevil Robertson. They were in the Range Rover edging back up the track and the tractor was disappearing towards Eton.

'Yes,' she said unsteadily.

He took one hand off the wheel and put it over her folded hands in her lap. 'All right?'

'Yes. No.' She sniffed again. 'I don't know why but I feel like crying actually.'

'Then cry.'

'No.' She laughed shakily. 'Don't mind me. I think it's just reaction and because I feel a bit foolish. I could never have coped with that alone.'

He said nothing, just squeezed her hands and concentrated on his driving until they reached the garden fence.

'Would you like to come in?' Kate said. 'You must be frozen and . . .'

'No. Thanks,' he interrupted, looking down at himself ruefully. 'I'd make too much of a mess. Anyway, you've managed to get wet, too, and you'll probably want to have a shower.'

This was true. Somehow or other the rain had seeped beneath her mackintosh and she'd lost her hat so that her hair was plastered wetly to her head, as his was. She looked across at him. He had turned the engine off and was facing towards her with one hand on the wheel, the other over the back of the seat.

She put a hand up and touched her hair; a droplet of water ran down her forehead and splashed on to her nose. And suddenly they were laughing together because they were in such a mess; it was a warm, wonderful feeling and . . .

Kate caught her breath and went to turn away but he said, 'I think we might have finally managed to break the ice, don't you, Kate? Should we cautiously make a pact to be friends from now on?'

She stared at him with her lips parted and her heart aching at what she saw, filled with the certain knowledge that just to be friends with him was going to hurt bitterly because she foolishly and hopelessly wanted so much more. What *is* it about him? she wondered fleetingly. His strength—she closed her eyes as she remembered watching him handle bits of timber and logs as if they were matchsticks—that air of authority and confidence, because he could be so nice when he chose?

'Kate?'

'Oh. Yes,' she said, but knew immediately that she had sounded strained and unsure. She tried to smile at him but that didn't come off too well, either.

'What is it?' he queried, his hazel eyes narrowed and suddenly very watchful.

'Nothing! Of course we can be friends.'

'Somehow, you don't quite convince me,' he said drily. 'What else have you got up your sleeve against me, Kate Wiley?'

'Not . . . not a thing,' she said jerkily and couldn't look at him. 'I'm so grateful . . . '

He swore. 'Here we go again. I don't believe it,' he said coldly.

Her eyes jerked to his face. 'No!' she protested. 'No, I . . . ' She put her hands to her mouth as he moved impatiently and started to speak, but something inside her gave way, a tiny sigh, a sense of inevitability, something that couldn't lie whatever the consequences, although she knew she would regret it. 'Do you remember what you said to me the other night?' she whispered.

He went still. 'About needing a man?'

She nodded.

'Yes, I do,' he said in a different voice. 'It was the other reason I came to see you today. To apologise. It was an unpleasant and unnecessary thing to have said.'

'It was also true.'

Their eyes clashed.

She licked her lips and went on very quietly, 'But not just any man—I've finally been able to work that out. Perhaps now you could understand how difficult this all is for me. I'm terribly sorry and I'm sure I'll get over it and I never ever intended to tell . . . to tell you,' her voice faltered for the first time, 'but the other way seemed to be so—I mean, after all you've done, well . . . ' She stopped.

The silence lengthened. Then he said very quietly, 'Oh, Kate . . . '

'No,' she broke in with sudden urgency, 'you don't have to say anything—please don't. I'll go now.' She fumbled for the door handle but he put a hand on her arm.

'Kate . . . '

'Please,' she whispered, 'just let me go.'

His eyes searched her pale face and darkened, deeply embarrassed eyes, then he took his hand away.

She slipped out into the rain and stumbled through the gate, through the garden and into the house without a backward glance.

CHAPTER FIVE

'Why do they have sports day in winter?' Serena grumbled.

'You say that every year,' Matt answered. 'And every year Mum tells you it's because it's too hot in summer.'

'I'd rather be too hot,' Serena said querulously.

Kate looked out of the window and found herself in secret agreement with Serena. Since the day her bridge had collapsed into the creek they had had two weeks of reasonable weather, then another week of rain. And although it wasn't actually raining on this annual school sports day, it was damp underfoot, overcast and chilly.

However, she coaxed Serena out of her blues and sent the two of them off, warmly wrapped up, to get the bus.

Even if it had been the most perfect day, she knew she would be looking forward to the sports with no more enthusiasm. She hadn't laid eyes on Grevil Robertson since that day, three weeks ago, when she had delivered her stunning news to him. But that, quite possibly was about to be altered today. Sports day was quite an event in the district and a lot of fathers and grandmothers and aunts and uncles generally attended.

If only I'd stopped to think, she chided herself, and not for the first time. It had been three weeks of mental torment for her; three weeks of feeling hot and cold whenever she thought of it, which was frequently. And experiencing an unpleasant hollow feeling at the pit of her stomach every time she wondered who in their right minds would tell that to a man they barely knew.

'Not that it makes much difference,' she murmured aloud. 'If I'd known him for years the facts of the matter are that I can't avoid seeing him for ever and he's engaged to someone else. What he must think of me, I can't imagine, and if all that's not bad enough, who is really to say it's not a sort of sexual frustration cropping up unexpectedly and he just had the misfortune to be on hand?'

And here I am, wondering how I could break a leg temporarily, she thought miserably, as she assembled all the goodies she had baked into tins. Well, Kate, you'll just have to grit your teeth and bear it, won't you? And you had better hurry up because you promised Marcie you'd be there by half past nine.

'Well, it hasn't actually rained yet, for which we should be grateful,' Marcie said fervently. 'Kate, I've put you down for the tea tent. Is that all right?'

'Fine! I'll get to work. Are the urns . . . ?'

'You OK?' Marcie interrupted.

Kate was tempted to lie but knew with Marcie it would be useless. So she lied all the same but in a different direction. 'I've got a headache but it will probably go once I get busy. Do I have an assistant?'

'May Watson has appointed herself to help you,' Marcie said out of the corner of her mouth. 'You know what she's like—she always picks her own jobs.'

Kate grimaced. 'But why me? I should have thought I'd be the last person in the world she would want to consort with.'

'I'd say she's bursting with curiosity.'

'What . . . You don't mean . . . '

'I do. Your association with the Robertsons. The fact that you actually got invited to tea, which improves your social standing dramatically. And by the way, I didn't say a word about anything! It must have been the bush telegraph.

Kate swore beneath her breath and Marcie laughed.

'I know how you feel, but in fact May is not the only one who's agog and dying to know all the details of your dealings with the Robertsons.

Kate closed her eyes and took several deep breaths but she left Marcie with a rueful grin. Although, as she made her way across the soggy sports ground which doubled as a cow paddock, she couldn't help sending up a prayer that the heavens would open up in a cloud burst.

The opposite occurred, as usual. As she and May Watson laid out a delicious array of the best of the district baking—plates piled high with rich brown coconut-dipped lamingtons; slices of cake: cherry, chocolate, fruit, angel, iced sponges, large cakes and cup cakes; spicy, homemade biscuits; sweet, sugary fudge; bright red toffee apples and cellophane packets of snowy popcorn—while they did this, the clouds rolled away and the sun shone.

'Well, Kate, I must say you look very nice today. New clothes?' May Watson enquired, as Kate set an enormous kettle on the gas bottle stove.

'Why yes, May,' Kate replied cheerfully, although she was cherishing uncharitable thoughts towards May Watson, wife of Les and mother of Stanley. May was about thirty-four and built along bulky, rather majestic lines although her bulk wasn't flabby. She never used any make-up and dressed very conservatively, but was not unattractive. 'As a matter of fact . . . ' I'll get this over and done with, Kate thought, 'I'm new from the skin out, May, and all thanks to the Robertsons. They've leased my river flats, did you know? Which effectively puts me back in business. They're both very nice, too, Grevil Robertson and his grandmother. They invited me over for tea. Have you met them yet, May?'

May Watson opened her mouth to speak but she was not a fool, whatever else you liked to think of her, Kate decided, as May closed her mouth and directed Kate a glance which clearly indicated she knew she was being mocked.

'No,' she said vaguely then, and turned away to rearrange the cups and saucers.

For a second, Kate felt guilty. After all, I don't have anything personal against May, she thought. Only her pompous husband and unpleasant child. On the other hand, she is domineering and gossipy and holds herself up as a pillar of society—not exactly a kindred spirit. And she must be aware of what Les says in front of Stanley. No, I think she had that coming!

And with a wry little smile, she suddenly discovered herself feeling somewhat brighter.

Things got busy from that point on. Although the sun was shining it was still cold and there was a brisk business in tea and coffee for the adults while they watched their offspring running and jumping and getting muddier and muddier, but loving every minute of it.

Then the children got their tea break and things were frantic for a while. But there was no sign of Grevil Robertson or his grandmother, nor any sign of them when she went over to the lunch tent later, to help out with the hot dogs and hamburgers.

He hasn't come, she thought with a sigh of relief, then felt a prickle of compunction for Tom. But she sighted him later, Tom, looking extremely happy and excited and obviously not missing his relatives.

Her day was further enhanced when Matt won the final of the long jump, beating several older boys, and Serena, who was not athletically inclined, ran up to him quite unaffectedly to hug him.

She went back to the tea tent after that to clear up. By the time she'd finished, most of the parents had left and the children would spend the last hour of the school day clearing the field before going home on the bus.

So it came as a shock to her as she made her way back to the truck, her arms full of cake tins, to bump into Grevil Robertson.

She stared up at him for one suspended moment, and would have given anything to be swallowed up in a convenient hole in the ground.

He said, 'Hello, Kate. Here, let me give you a hand.'

'No, thanks, I'll be fine,' she answered awkwardly and immediately dropped a tin. She closed her eyes in horrible frustration. But she managed to compose herself as he bent to retrieve the tin, and to say, 'I thought you hadn't come. I didn't see you earlier.'

'No. Unfortunately I was held up in Brisbane this morning and my grandmother has a cold. But I did make it in time to see Tom receive a ribbon. By the way, I'm parked next to you so if you give me a couple of those it would lighten your load.'

Kate hesitated, then did so, and they started to walk towards the cars. She had not looked at him fully since that first look but her heart was bumping uncomfortably.

'By the look of things,' he said, 'Tom has fitted in well.'

'Yes, I'd say he has. But then he's a nice kid.' She bit her lip and was conscious of Grevil Robertson glancing sideways at her as they skirted a patch of mud. They came up to the cars then and Kate dumped her cargo noisily into the back of the ute, accepted the other tins and dropped them in, too, and dug into her pocket for keys, not knowing what to do or say next.

'Kate,' he said quietly.

She bowed her head briefly, took a deep breath and turned to face him. 'Don't say anything, please,' she muttered and was horrified to find her voice unsteady and on the verge of tears.

'I must say this.' She was turning her keys over and over agitatedly and he put out a hand to take them from her. 'Of all the things I value in a person,' he went on, 'honesty comes at the top of the list.'

Kate winced. 'All the same, I'm sure you could have done without that kind of honesty. I know I

could, now. I feel incredibly foolish and anyway,'
her voice sank, 'I'm not even sure if it was the truth.'
She looked away. 'I mean, I've had time to think
about it.' She shrugged helplessly.

'I know,' he said after a moment. 'So have I. And
my guess is that you'll wake up one morning and
wonder who the hell Grevil Robertson was—in this
context. You see, I've been through this myself. The
re-awakening process. I know how painful and
confusing it can be.'

Kate lifted suddenly wide grey eyes to his. 'Is this
how it happened for you?' she asked shakily. 'An—
irrational sort of impulse?'

A smile lit his eyes and Kate flushed. 'I didn't
mean it to sound like that.'

'I know what you meant. Yes it did.'

'What did you do about it?' This time she blushed
to the roots of her hair as the words left her mouth,
and she turned away clumsily, conscious of having
been unpardonably personal.

But he put his hands on her shoulders and turned
her back. 'Kate,' he said deliberately and paused,
his hazel eyes searching her hot, distressed face, 'not
what *you* should do about it. I went from one bed
to another but, believe me, that's not the answer.'

'You said . . . that night you said . . . ' she
whispered and stopped.

'What I said that night was uttered in the heat of
the moment and I very much regret it.'

'Other people have said it to me.'

'It's become a well-known platitude,' he said
drily. 'But I can assure you, it only affords you
temporary relief and then it leaves you disliking
yourself.'

'I didn't know men thought that way.'

'Why shouldn't they?' he asked. 'If you've been happy with someone, in love, and then they're gone, you know what the real thing is and a substitute for it isn't good enough, whether you're a man or a woman.'

Kate stared up at him a little wonderingly. 'All you've said is what I've told myself,' she said huskily. 'I wasn't really planning to go out and . . . ' She shrugged.

'I know that.'

'How?' she asked with a tinge of bitterness. 'I couldn't blame you for thinking I was a real idiot, if nothing else.'

'I never thought that. Just someone struggling with intolerably heavy burdens. And now this, which has made you angry with yourself and guilt-ridden and ashamed . . . '

'Not only that,' she broke in, 'but so ridiculous as to try to transfer all my anger to you.'

'You're being too hard on yourself, Kate,' he said with a gentleness that caused tears to prick her eyelids. 'It's all a very natural and human process. You wake up suddenly and realise you're a member of the human race again, and you begin to think and look around and contemplate building another life. And you make mistakes like everyone else does, but you're a bit more vulnerable to it because of a special kind of loneliness. And that's what you have to guard against.'

Kate was silent for a time, looking across the sports ground lying empty now and dotted with the shadows of some high, white, rounded cloud. Then she said, 'I'm so glad it's worked out for you, that you've found someone. And I can't help thinking that she must be very lucky. It's strange,' she went on quickly. 'We barely know each other in some ways and to be honest, for the past three weeks I've been wondering whether I should go out and shoot myself—well, not only the last three weeks. I've felt there wasn't much purpose to life for quite a time now. But right now, I feel as if I just might survive. Thanks to you.'

It was his turn to be silent. In fact he leant back against the Range Rover with his arms folded and studied her contemplatively until she looked away awkwardly and wondered what was coming next.

He surprised her. 'Do you know what I would like?' he said, not quite smiling.

'No . . . '

'I'd like to think that you felt you knew me well enough now to dispense with all the sentiments of gratitude, obligation and appreciation.' He straightened.

She went red, then found herself laughing. 'All right. All the same, if I can't say it perhaps I can show it.' And on an impulse, she stood up tall and kissed him fleetingly on the lips, only to be immediately stricken with remorse. 'I—I only meant that,' she stammered, 'as . . . '

'Oh, Kate,' he laughed, and folded her into his arms, 'of course. But that doesn't mean to say I can't return the compliment.' And he kissed her back.

It was only as she was driving away that Kate realised that the solitary car left beside the paddock was May Weston's, and that May was sitting in it, ostentatiously fiddling with her seatbelt.

'Damn!' Kate muttered. 'How long has she been sitting there spying on me?'

She slept well that night for the first time for weeks and the next morning discovered that she felt as if she'd recovered from a fever. A little shaky physically, but as if the corners of her mind had been taken out and dusted, and as if life was a bright, white sheet she might write on again.

She also decided to take Mrs Robertson's advice about getting out and about more and was presented with an opportunity to do so that very morning.

There was just a faint touch of spring in the air and Marcie arrived to visit her wearing a tennis skirt over tracksuit trousers.

The local tennis circuit was actually a social round of the ladies of the district, where a good gossip was as important as the game, and once a month a mixed tennis party was thrown on a Sunday. Until Mike had died, Kate had played once a week and enjoyed it and their court had always been in tip-top condition. Some time after his death she had tried to take up the threads again, of sociability and tennis, but found she'd had no heart for it. There were also, she had discovered, certain pitfalls to the mixed social side of it. As if I'd want any of their husbands, she had marvelled once. What do they think I am?

But when, on that early spring morning, she said something to Marcie about being game to take up tennis so soon in the season and when Marcie, by way of reply, suggested she go too, she stopped and thought about it and found she'd like nothing so much as a good game of tennis.

But she hesitated. 'I haven't played for years, Marcie.'

'Kate, anyone as good as you were isn't going to forget the game. You may be a little rusty for a while but one thing in your favour, you're as fit as a fiddle.'

Kate grimaced. Then she said slowly, 'I was thinking of getting the court fixed up. It seems such a shame to have let it go to ruin.'

'Great! An extra court is a bonus. It varies the scenery,' Marcie said humorously. Then she tilted her head to one side to do some mental arithmetic. 'Let's see, that would bring the total up to eight in the district, which means you'd only have to hold it here once every two months for the ladies and once every eight months for the mixed day.'

'Uh-huh. I don't know about the mixed days, Marcie.'

'Why not?'

'I found them a special trial after Mike died. You know, wives looking at me as if I was some kind of a predator.' She stopped and bit her lip but went on hastily, 'And husbands, some of them, with a certain speculative little look in their eyes.'

'Kate,' Marcie said softly, 'that's the way of the world, I guess. But who cares about those kind of people? Don't shut yourself away because of them.'

'No. No, you're right,' Kate said slowly. 'OK!'

So she dug out a tennis dress and while she ironed it, Marcie sat at her kitchen table and chatted.

'By the way, I've been meaning to ask you this, Kate. Did you know that Grevil Robertson is getting married again?'

'Yes, I did. His grandmother told me.'

'You didn't mention it,' Marcie said a shade reproachfully. 'Come to that, you were extremely cagey about your visit to Eton altogether!'

Kate smiled faintly. 'That's because I'm eating humble pie. I enjoyed myself, contrary to expectation, and I thought Mrs Robertson was very nice.'

'And Mr Robertson?' Marcie asked tentatively.

Kate looked away but said perfectly normally, 'I've had to revise my opinions about him, Marcie. He's actually very nice, too.' She looked back at Marcie with her grey eyes twinkling. 'Now don't you dare say I told you so.'

'Wouldn't dream of it,' Marcie declared. 'But I am happy to hear it. Apparently the wedding has had to be postponed. The bride-to-be's father has been very ill. However, and this is the real titbit, he's out of danger now although still bed-ridden and she's coming to spend a week at Eton,' Marcie finished with a flourish.

'How nice,' Kate murmured and held her tennis dress up for inspection.

'But you're not interested?'

Kate looked at her ruefully. 'Are you?'

'Of course I am,' Marcie said honestly. 'I mean, it's like having a royal family in our midst, the Robertsons! Anyway, I'm only talking facts, Kate Wiley, whereas I could be imparting to you all the speculation which is buzzing around the place, but of course I won't sully your ears with it.' She cocked an eyebrow at Kate and added softly, 'Or should I?'

Kate was tempted to say briskly, no don't, but realised it would be falling into a trap of her own making. Marcie was no fool and she knew that Kate wasn't normally averse to a bit of clean gossip. 'You might as well,' she said wryly.

Marcie ticked off her fingers, 'She's from another prominent grazing family, she's known him nearly all her life, she's very young and very lovely, of course . . . '

'Of course,' Kate echoed with an unexpected tinge of irony, and to cover her tracks said, 'But aren't we still dealing in facts? What's the speculation about?'

'I was coming to that,' Marcie said patiently. 'Apparently Grevil Robertson hasn't exactly lived like a monk since his first wife died . . . ' She broke off and eyed Kate expectantly as if expecting *her* to say, I told you so.

But all she said was, 'So?'

'Well, it's led some good people to wonder why he's taking a very young bride.'

'How old?'

'Just twenty, apparently,' Marcie said. 'The other thing some people see as strange is the long engagement which, admittedly, has gone out of vogue these days.'

'Her father has been very ill.'

'That's what I thought, but someone put forward the theory in that case he'd be happy to know his only daughter was safely wedded, and they could have taken the wedding to his bedside. But perhaps she wants a wedding she'll remember all her life. Oh, really,' Marcie waved a hand and did look a bit guilty then, 'it's nobody's business but their own.'

'Amen,' Kate said quietly. 'Twenty . . . That's not so young though, is it? I was nineteen.'

'No,' Marcie agreed, 'but he's thirty-nine. It's a big age difference, I guess. Mind you, I hope they live happily after because I *like* Grevil Robertson. Kate, are you going to wear that dress or stand there holding it up all day?'

'Wear it!' Kate replied and went off to get changed.

The next month saw Kate's life take a turn for the better. Just the simple action of going to tennis again seemed to release some bonds she hadn't been aware of and, in spite of herself, she enjoyed it. She also got her tennis court resurfaced and netted and spent an hour each day hitting up against the practice wall. She'd been a school champion at tennis and as all her old skills started to come back, she thought often of her father, who had so wanted her to be everything that was feminine, and had got instead a daughter who could outride, outswim and outplay on a tennis court a lot of men.

On the other hand, she had stopped to think once, what is femininity? Mike used to be able to make me feel the essence of it, although I could beat him at tennis.

But all in all, she didn't have much time for random thoughts of this nature; she was too busy. She was not only working around the property with renewed energy and enthusiasm and a real desire to get it back to how it had looked when Mike had been alive—she'd employed some help—but she'd also rejoined the Toowoomba library and enrolled for a pottery course at the Darling Downs Institute of Advanced Education, known affectionately as the DDIAE.

She didn't see Grevil at all.

Then one morning Mrs Robertson descended on her out of the blue with a proposal that momentarily pierced asunder the bright white sheet of life she thought she was rewriting so well.

'My dear Katherine, you do look well. Sorry to be dropping in on you like this and you've probably wondered why you haven't heard from me for ages, but I've been in Sydney—am I forgiven?'

'Of course! Anyway it was my turn, Mrs Robertson. Come in and sit down. You're looking very well yourself.'

'Why, thank you, my dear. Actually, I've come to enlist your aid!' But before she explained herself as Kate settled her in the lounge, she enquired what Kate had been doing with herself and, when told, expressed delight.

'That's the spirit! And see what it's done for you; you're looking so attractive. Not only that but it fits in so perfectly. Oh, I am pleased with you!'

Kate had to smile although she didn't understand what fitted in so perfectly. Five minutes later she did, and found it much harder to smile.

'You want me to help you organise a tennis party to welcome Grevil's fiancée to the district?' she said slowly and with a sinking feeling at the pit of her stomach.

'Don't you think it's a good idea, Katherine? She—her name is Jennifer—is coming up to spend a week with us. She was due several weeks ago but her father had a slight setback. And I mean, once she's married to Grevil, she'll be spending her life here, more or less, so why not start to get to know everyone now? It's the way we used to do things in the dim, distant days of my youth,' she said humorously, 'and anyway, I must confess, *I* would like to get to know some people around. I'm that sort of a person, Katherine. I thrive on knowing people.'

Kate could believe this easily but all she could think of to say, was, 'Does she play tennis?'

'Of course. Would I suggest it otherwise?'

'No. Well, I'm sure the ladies of the district would be delighted. Er . . . what about the ones who don't play tennis?

'Rome wasn't built in a day,' Mrs Robertson said wisely. 'One has to start somewhere. As a matter of fact, I did think,' she added a shade wistfully, 'of a garden party. But that has a ring of grandeur to it and we Robertsons have never had any truck with delusions of grandeur. Besides, I felt everyone might feel obliged to dash out and buy a new hat.'

For a moment Kate's sense of humour emerged as she visualised just that and thought, for that matter, that even a tennis party at Eton was going to cause a few flutters.

'Katherine?'

'Oh. Sorry,' Kate said gathering her mental processes but with a feeling of doom.

'Don't you think it's a good idea?'

'I . . . yes!'

'Then you won't mind helping me to organise it, my dear?'

'No.'

'Oh, good. I knew I could count on you! Let's discuss dates, etc, now.'

'All right,' Kate said helplessly. 'Would you like a cup of tea?'

'Love one,' Mrs Robertson said with relish.

Kate rose. 'What does Grevil think of the idea?'

'He doesn't know about it. He's been away, too— he's bringing Jennifer back with him. But Grevil generally goes along with my ideas,' his grandmother said confidently.

That night, Kate forced herself to examine truthfully her feelings about the tennis party and that one dizzying moment when the thought of having to meet Grevil's future wife had been like a curious form of torture.

'But perhaps it's what I need to deliver the *coup de grâce* to any lingering doubts I have on the subject,' she whispered to herself. 'And perhaps it's best to get it over and done with,' she mused. 'I'm not going to be able to avoid her for ever. Only, I have the horrible feeling Mrs Robertson might expect us to become friends. Which would be the height of irony, wouldn't it? Oh, damn. And I was going so well, too.'

°10 'Hello, Mrs Wiley,' Tom Robertson said enthusiastically over the counter of the school tuckshop.

'Hello, Tom! What can I do for you?'

Tom pulled a scrap of paper from his pocket and handed it to her. 'I'm collecting the teacher's little lunch today,' he said importantly. 'Dad's home, Mrs Wiley,' he added enthusiastically. 'And Jenny, too.'

'That's great, Tom. Let's see.' She started to collect a selection of buns and biscuits.

Because it was a small school, the tuckshop was only run once a week and was manned and stocked by mothers. It was Kate's turn to work today with two other mothers and, because the tennis party was only two days away, the other two mothers, both tennis players, were in a mood of pleasurable anticipation.

'He's a honey,' Louise Bass said to Kate, as Tom departed with a wave and Kate waved back. 'I must say I'm really looking forward to meeting the Robertsons and seeing Eton. I just hope the excitement doesn't affect my tennis too drastically!' she added wryly.

'I'm sure it won't,' Kate murmured.

'You are . . . You are going, aren't you, Kate?'

Kate looked up, startled. 'Yes. Why not?'

'Oh . . . ' Louise looked uncomfortable suddenly. 'It was just something May Watson said,' she mumbled.

Kate felt her hackles rise immediately, but she said quite calmly, 'What did she say?'

'Well,' Louise Bass twisted a tea towel between her fingers and her expression clearly indicated the fact that she was mentally kicking herself. Kate didn't know her very well but had always found her easy to get along with. 'Well, she said, "I'd be surprised if Kate has the gall to go".' The words came out in a rush and the other girl's cheeks were pink as she added, 'I asked her what she meant but she just gave me that basilisk stare she does so well.'

Kate was silent, her lips tight.

'I'm sorry, Kate,' Louise said timidly. 'I don't know what on earth made me ask you. I don't even like May that much, she . . . well . . . But then

I've always had the problem of speaking before I stop to think,' she said miserably.

Kate stared at her and decided she was genuinely one of those unfortunate people. And after all, who am I to be superior about it, she thought mockingly.

'Don't worry about it, Louise,' she said mildly. As for May bloody Watson, she would have liked to add but didn't, saying instead musingly, 'Basilisk . . . what a lovely word!'

Then they were both laughing, Louise with some relief.

But a tiny flame of anger had begun to burn within Kate which was one day to have disastrous results.

That same afternoon she ran into Grevil Robertson.

She had decided to go down and have a look at the old shearing shed. She and Mike had never run sheep but the previous owners of Kunnunurra had, and won many awards for their wool. It had occurred to her that it might be a profitable diversification, and an interesting one, too, although she'd only be able to start off in a small way.

Because it was a beautiful spring day, she decided to ride down rather than drive, a thing she had got out of the habit of doing during the harsh winter months—a thing her horse had got out of the habit of as well. Although he allowed himself to be caught easily enough, he gave clear indication once she was mounted that he had considered himself retired to the paddock for life.

'We'll see about that!' Kate said to him and whistled for Digby, came accompanied by the goat.

True to her word, Kate had banished the goat from the garden and he had since been tethered on a long line on a different patch of grass each day, within reach of shade, and stabled every night.

Kate eyed him. 'I suppose you've eaten through your rope again, you insufferable animal!' But because it was a lovely day and the air smelt sweet and heavy with grass seed, she added, 'Oh, well, you can come too.' And wondered with a grin how many people went riding with a mad pet goat.

Not that she had either the goat's or the dog's company for long. Digby employed a time-honoured ploy. He raced ahead several times, barking excitedly and then stopping and looking back at Kate almost humanly. And when she didn't whistle him back at all, he took it to mean that this excursion was a fun thing and not work, and he disappeared to chase hares, which he never caught. The goat looked almost humanly undecided for a time, too, then, possibly recalling that he wasn't exactly a favoured companion of Kate's, disappeared as well.

The shearing shed was in worse disrepair than Kate had imagined, although the electric combing equipment was packed away safely. She tethered her horse just inside the shed and made her inspection on foot. It was a wooden building with a steeply sloping roof but many of the roofing panels were rusted and had holes in them and the grey, weathered old timber of the walls was showing sign of rot.

'I wonder,' she mused as she trod carefully along the raised platform where the shearing was actually done and the shorn sheep passed down chutes through the wall to the yards outside, 'if it's worth it?'

She looked around. One end of the shed was open and she could imagine the wind whistling through, and whistling through the holes in the roof. She shivered suddenly and decided it was an eerie place and, all in all, she might think again about sheep.

It was then that she heard a sound and noticed her horse prick up its ears and stir restlessly.

'What was that?' she muttered, and the sound came again, a clink of metal against rock.

For some extraordinary reason she felt herself go cold with fear and found herself clutching a wooden railing as the horse stood quite still but with its nostrils quivering, its head poised alertly.

Then it reared up and whinnied loudly. The sound reverberated and crashed around the roof, and Grevil Robertson rode into the shed. Kate closed her eyes and swayed on suddenly unsteady legs.

He rode right up to where she was standing on the platform, still clutching the rail as if her life depended on it.

'I saw you from across the creek,' he said. 'Kate? Are you all right?'

She swallowed and forcibly uncurled her fingers from the railing so she could wipe the sudden dewing of sweat from her brow. 'Fine,' she said weakly.

'You don't look it.'

'I . . . God knows why but you gave me an awful fright,' she confessed. 'I'd just decided this place gave me the willies when I heard—it must have been your horse's shoe clinking on a rock. I don't know what I expected but it wasn't you,' she said ruefully.

'I'll have to get out of the habit of catching you unawares.'

'I think it was more me, but I'm not usually nervy or over-imaginative.'

He looked around and smiled slightly. 'It's the kind of place you could expect bats and rats to lurk. If you're frightened of them it would be easy to associate the place with more sinister things.'

'You're right,' Kate said with a shiver, and made to jump down from the platform.

But he said with a curious abruptness, 'How are you otherwise?'

She straightened and would have given anything to be able to pretend to herself and him that she didn't know perfectly well what he meant. To be able to pretend that it was just a polite enquiry and to be able to answer it mundanely and politely. But by once speaking openly to this tall man who sat his horse so easily and was watching her so carefully, she had surrendered the right to play games with words. At least, she thought wretchedly, it's a choice between being dishonest and making a fool of myself or being honest—and making a fool of myself.

'I'm coping,' she said quietly.

'Kate . . . '

'Grevil,' she interrupted, and thought how few times she'd called him that, 'I think we said it all the last time we met. Have you . . . Did you want to see me about something?'

'Yes. This bloody tennis party. My beloved grandmother,' he said grimly, 'is . . . '

'Was not to know,' Kate said quietly.

'She should have consulted me first. She takes too much upon herself sometimes.'

Kate was silent. Then she said with an effort, 'Everyone is looking forward to it so much.'

'Bar you.'

'Bar me,' she conceded, staring down at her hands. 'But I'll manage. I even thought it might be a good idea to get it over and done with.' She looked up, straight into his eyes, and managed to smile faintly. 'Does she—Jennifer—like it up here?'

'Yes, she seems to.'

'I'm glad,' Kate said quietly and jumped down. But as she swung herself into the saddle, her stupid horse chose that moment to make his resentment felt once more and he reared high again with the prime intention of dislodging her.

A hard hand shot out and Grevil stood up in his stirrups and dragged the horse down by its bridle and held his head while Kate recovered herself.

'I got him out of the paddock today so he's really fresh,' she said breathlessly. 'Thank you.'

He let go of the bridle and they walked their horses out of the shed side by side, their legs brushing.

Kate caught her breath and said the first thing that came to mind. 'I've got a goat and a dog somewhere, chasing hares.' She looked around and spotted Digby halfway up the hillside, but of Billy the goat there was no sign.

'A goat?' Grevil queried.

'Yes. I should have got rid of him ages ago. He's a very naughty goat. In fact I shudder to think of what he's up to now that he's loose—I bet he's gone straight home to the washing line,' she said with sudden and genuine indignation.

'I had a pet goat as a child,' Grevil said with a grin. 'His speciality was jumping into cars and tearing the stuffing out of the seats.'

'Thank heavens Billy hasn't thought of that— yet! I'd better go though.'

'Will you be all right?' He looked down at her questioningly.

'Oh, yes!' She patted her horse's neck. 'He's not a bad old nag really.' She stopped, not sure suddenly if that was what he'd meant.

But he smiled down at her and said gently, 'See you, then,' and wheeled his horse away.

It was only as she was half-way up the hill at a canter that Kate realised her cheeks wer wet with tears. Perhaps it would be easier to rid oneself of an irrational sort of impulse if you weren't constantly being confronted with the personification, she thought miserably, and licked the saltiness off her lips. I just *hope* we're both right about this—this reawakening bit—because if not . . .

She shivered inwardly and tightened her fingers around the reins and recalled that it had taken her no time at all to fall deeply in love with Mike.

'And if that's how it's happened for me again . . . Oh, *hell!* And I thought I was going so well.'

That evening she found that even at home she couldn't escape Grevil Robertson.

Serena had to deliver a talk the next morning, and was wading laboriously through the newspaper in search of a subject. Kate hadn't read the paper but they were sitting in the lounge; at least, Kate was, mending some clothes and making suggestions while Serena lay on the floor with the paper spread out in front of her.

'What about . . . '

'Mum,' Serena interrupted. 'guess who's in the paper?'

'Who?'

'Tom's dad. Look, there's a picture of him, and one of Eton.'

'So there is,' Kate tried to say lightly as she bent over to have a look.

'You know, I like him,' Serena said. 'He doesn't make a fuss even though he is the richest person around.'

'Mr Robertson?' Matt asked coming in from his bath looking all pink and scrubbed.

'Is your hair dry, love?' Kate asked.

'Nearly. A lot of people like him, you know.'

'Get me a towel, Matt, and I'll dry it properly for you.'

But Matt was not to be deterred as he knelt in front of her and had his hair vigorously towelled. 'I heard Whitney Wainright's father saying so to Mr Hunter the other day. He said he was a really decent bloke.'

'There,' Kate said, as Matt emerged from the folds of the towel looking pinker than ever and with his short dark hair standing up in peaks.

Serena propped her small chin on her hands and stared into the fire and said presently, 'If you *had* to have a father, I wouldn't mind having one like Mr Robertson.'

After they'd gone to bed, Kate read the article then sat for a long time with the paper in her lap, staring at it. The article was mainly a résumé of Grevil Robertson's life, his distinguished school and university career—he was a Bachelor of Science and had played first grade cricket—how he'd weathered a major drought as a grazier and how he was now diversifying into grain.

The picture of him seemed to capture it all, she thought; a clever, resourceful man who knew how to wield his wealth and power lightly.

He's even managed to impress Serena, she thought with a faint sad smile, and shivered in spite of the fire because the night had gone suddenly cold.

CHAPTER SIX

'NEITHER flood nor pestilence . . . my God, I'm going biblical again,' Kate said to herself on the morning of the tennis party as she looked out on a calm, gentle spring day.

She was ready to leave. She wore a pale green knitted shirt and a short white skirt, matching green socks and snowy white tennis shoes. The weeks of reasonable weather had given her skin a faint golden bloom and brought out the russet highlights in her hair.

She looked good, she decided: slim about the waist, long-legged and with the curve of her bosom showing up nicely beneath the shirt. Then she turned away from the shadows she saw in her grey eyes and took several deep breaths.

She picked up her racquet and white jumper, her purse, and sallied forth.

At three o'clock, she returned, put her racquet away carefully, changed out of her tennis gear and started to make tea for Serena and Matt with careful deliberation.

'How was it, Mum?' Matt asked bursting into the kitchen excitedly. 'Did you clobber 'em?'

'I hope not,' Kate said with a grin.

'Tell us about it, Mum,' Serena begged.

'Well,' Kate put a plate of sandwiches on the table and two glasses of milk, and sat down to pour herself a cup of tea, 'the food was magnificent. We had morning tea in the little pavilion beside the court and lunch on the front veranda—cold chicken and turkey, salmon mousse, fresh asparagus and salads, strawberries and cream. And we played a sort of round-robin competition.'

'Did you win?' Matt asked through mouthfuls of Marmite sandwich.

'Don't talk with your mouth full, love. No. But I got to the final of the singles and . . . '

'Who beat you?' Serena looked disappointed. 'I thought you were supposed to be the best around here.'

'Um, Tom's new mother. But Marcie and I won the doubles.'

'Oh, well,' Serena brightened, 'that's not so bad I suppose. Tom really likes her. He says it will be more like having an older sister than a mother. Her name is Jenny—of course old Mrs Robertson doesn't call her that,' she said with a giggle. 'Did she play?'

'She's too old!' Matt said. 'Isn't she, Mum?'

'Yes,' Kate said musingly, 'but I think she must have been rather good once. She knew what she was talking about.'

'Was Stanley Watson's mum there?' Serena asked.

Kate put her cup down. 'Yes. Why do you ask?'

'She told Stanley she mightn't go.'

'Oh? Why not?'

'He wouldn't tell us, not properly. But I think it must have had something to do with you. Until you started to play again, she was the best.'

This was true, Kate knew. Despite her bulk, May Watson was surprisingly light on her surprisingly dainty feet. And she had good ground strokes and the ability not to get ruffled. That she might have resented surrendering or having to share he supremacy was something that had not occurred to Kate.

But it should have, Kate mused, because for some insane reason, May and I seemed to be locked on a collision course.

'What really made you think Stanley's mum wouldn't go because of me, Serena? He must have said something else.'

Serena looked uncomfortable. 'I . . . ' she began. 'Well, we were talking about the tennis party and I said you would win for sure . . . '

'Serena!'

'Was it such a bad thing to say? If you can't boast a bit about your own mum, who can you boast about?' She stared at Kate out of Mike's eyes, which had been capable of looking amazingly stubborn at times, too.

'Darling, it's a little unwise to make rash statements like that, but thank you for your confidence.' She smiled at Serena. 'I'm only sorry I disappointed you, but go on.'

'Well, Stanley said the only reason you would win was because his mum might not be there and I said, is she frightened of playing my mum?'

Oh, dear, Kate thought, how to deal with this? 'That wasn't a very nice thing to say, was it?'

'I suppose not,' Serena said grudgingly, 'but Stanley is usually the first to start things.'

'That's true,' Matt agreed.

'What did Stanley say then?' Kate enquired with a feeling of fatal fascination.

'He said the only thing his mum was frightened of was you making a fool of yourself. But I knew he'd made that up because he couldn't think of anything else to say, so I laughed and he walked away in a temper.'

Kate stared at her daughter, unwilling to believe her ears, because she didn't at all share Serena's conviction that Stanley had made it up. It fitted in too well with what his mother had said to Louise Bass and stemmed, undoubtedly, from what May had witnessed after the sports day and totally misinterpreted. Well . . . But surely she doesn't *say* these things to Stanley? He must overhear her . . .

'Serena,' she said abruptly, 'this little feud between you and Stanley Watson has gone on long enough. Now I understand that you would have been happy and proud for me to win the tennis today, but I don't want you ever to get into any more slanging matches with him.'

'What's a slanging match?'

Kate counted to ten. 'Saying things that are unkind and personal.'

'What if he starts it?'

'You are to turn around and walk away from him. Now I *mean* that.'

'Don't punch him either, Mum means,' Matt offered and they both giggled, but tailed off at the unusually stern look on Kate's face.

Serena hesitated then she said, 'OK, I'll try.'

'That's not good enough. You'll do it. And so will you, Matt. And I expect you to back Serena up—

it's over and finished, all this nonsense,' Kate said
with quiet but steely emphasis. But her heart was
raw and angry as she said it because over and above
wanting to stamp out something that was getting
out of hand, who was to say what Serena might hear
from Stanley Watson, who was obviously privy,
wittingly or unwittingly, to his mother's malicious
gossip.

'I promise,' Serena said a little tearfully then, and
came to put her arms around Kate's waist. 'I'm
sorry, Mum.'

Kate stared down at the dark silky head then she
knelt down and took Serena in her arms. 'It's all
right, love,' she said huskily.

Kate stirred and sighed. She was sitting curled up
in a lounge chair by the light of a fire and pondering
one of the stranger days of her life.

Curiouser and curiouser it all gets, she thought.
Grevil is marrying a lovely . . . child.

A vivid mental picture of Jennifer Kent, soon to
be Robertson, presented itself to her. Quite tall with
a rounded figure that seemed to suggest it hadn't
quite fined down from girlhood to womanhood yet;
dark blue eyes and wavy fair hair, a shy, lovely
smile, beautiful manners and something in those
blue eyes—a blend of nervousness, a desire to please
and a hint of a sunny, happy nature—that had quite
taken the ladies of the tennis circuit by storm.

And Mrs Robertson, as proud as if this was her
own daughter.

'. . . What do you think of her, Katherine?' she asked, taking Kate aside while Jennifer was on the court.

'She's lovely,' Kate said sincerely.

'I think so, too. I'm so happy for Grevil.' Mrs Robertson blinked unashamedly. 'After all he's been through, he deserves it.' Kate must have looked enquiring because Mrs Robertson went on, 'I don't suppose you know this but Solange died as a direct result of having Tom—well, they discovered she had a rare blood disease and no one knew what effect pregnancy would have on her. But she was quite determined to have a baby even it killed her—which it did. Of course Grevil could never regret Tom, but at the same time it was hard not to blame himself.'

'I didn't know,' Kate said very quietly, thinking with an inner tremor of the extra burden of pain Grevil Robertson had borne.

'That's why I'm so determined to give this marriage every chance,' Mrs Robertson said with a return of her normal vigour. 'For some obscure reason, Grevil was quite cross with me about this party. But I said to him exactly what I said to you— and fortunately, it was too late to cancel then without it all looking very odd. Perhaps it was because Jennifer is a little shy, but on the other hand, she's had an excellent upbringing and I think she's coping brilliantly. By the way, I know I can count on you to be a friend to her, Katherine.'

'Of course.'

'What do you think of her, Kate?' This was Marcie, *sotto voce*, during the tea break.

'She's a lovely . . . ' Kate bit her lip.

'Child?'

'I didn't . . . I mean . . . '

'I thought so, too,' Marcie said with a grin. 'But it's a well-known fact that very experienced men often fall for girlish innocence, I guess.'

' . . . Well, what do you think of her, Kate?'

Kate lifted her head and stared at May Watson over a plate of chicken and salad. 'I'm really looking forward to having her as a neighbour and a friend, May,' she said perfectly steadily. 'What do you think of her?'

May shrugged and murmured something non-committal.

'And it's just as well,' Kate said to the fire, coming back to the present, 'that I wasn't aware then of what Stanley said to Serena or I might have poured chicken salad all over you, May.'

But really, the only possible thing I can do about May, she thought then as she stared into the flames, is take my own advice to Serena.

She traced a pattern on the arm of the chair with one finger, wishing she could blank out her mind, but the rest of the tennis party would not let her go.

'I've heard so much about you, Mrs Wiley,' Jennifer Kent had said with that lovely, shy smile. 'And about Serena and Matt. I'd love to have twins.'

Kate had had a bitter-sweet vision of this girl heavy with Grevil's baby but had managed to say laughingly, 'That's asking for double trouble, but please call me Kate. Everyone does except,' she lowered her voice, 'Mrs Robertson.'

'If you'll call me Jenny,' Jennifer had said with a grin and added, 'But Grandmama Robertson says you are her ideal kind of woman—resourceful, independent, but feminine all the same. That's how I'd like to be.'

And how could I resist that? Kate thought, sitting huddled in her chair, staring into the firelight. Is that why I let her win the tennis? Did I do that? Yes. She's good, but . . . And unfortunately Mrs Robertson realised what I'd done because she said to me with a twinkle in her eye, that was very kind of you, Kate. Only it wasn't kindness, it was the sudden conviction I had that beating her was like saying, if I can't measure up in any other way, at least I can do this better. Reverse psychology? Something like that. Then Grevil arrived . . .

She closed her eyes and laid her cheek against the chair with another vivid little mental picture engraved upon her mind. Of Jennifer looking oddly flustered as Grevil had strolled across the lawn towards them. As if she didn't quite know how to handle greeting him in front of a bevy of strange ladies. Of how she had looked up at him gravely but faintly pink-cheeked and how he had kissed her briefly on the lips, then taken her hand reassuringly and then Mrs Robertson had taken over like a stage manager directing events—introductions all round and Grevil taking it all in his stride, even the ones who had simpered and probably hated themselves for it, but that was the effect of him . . . Of herself saying brightly, I've had a lovely day. Thank you so much. You must come and see me if you get a chance before you go back . . .

'What else could I say?' she whispered. 'What else can I do?'

Two things happened over the next week to take Kate's mind off certain things. She met an old friend of Mike's and she nearly killed a man.

She had spent the morning at her pottery class and was in Toowoomba doing some shopping when a voice from the past said her name and she turned to see a tall dark man looking at her with surprised recognition.

'Jim Compton!' she said. 'Is it really you?'

He laughed. 'Really me, Kate. I haven't seen you for years. Not since Mike . . . ' He broke off.

'Mike died,' Kate supplied. 'But what are you doing here? I thought you'd gone to live in Papua New Guinea.'

'I've come back, Kate. To start up my own crop-spraying business. But look, can I buy you lunch?'

'That would be lovely,' Kate said.

They found a quiet little restaurant and spent a pleasurable hour and a half swapping recent histories. Jim was a pilot and had been a friend of Mike's when he'd been employed in the area by a crop-spraying firm. Kate had always liked his quiet way and the flashes of humour that lit up his blue eyes. He told her that his years in Papua New Guinea had provided the capital for his new business and Kate judged, reading between the lines, that the hazardous flying conditions up there had provided him with an excellent reputation as a pilot.

'And you've never married?' she asked.

'No.' He grinned. 'Never found anyone to take me on.'

'Oh, Jim, I think it's more than you're a loner at heart!'

'Perhaps,' he admitted and looked suddenly sober as he said, 'Kate, I should have been to see you—not that I've been back that long—but quite honestly I assumed that you would have sold up after Mike's death.'

'Perhaps it's what I should have done,' she said a shade drily.

'Not if you've made a go of it.'

'Well,' she hesitated, 'I've had some help. Things were a bit desperate for a while but now . . . ' She shrugged.

'And you've never thought of remarrying?' he asked quietly.

'Oh, I've thought of it,' she said and smiled at him. 'Perhaps one day.'

He smiled gently back at her and she felt flooded with warmth. And perhaps it was that warmth that led her into what turned out to be an awkward situation.

Jim went on to ask her what kind of help she'd had and she told him about Eton leasing her river flats.

'Ah, Eton,' he said a shade wistfully. 'I wish I had an in there. If I could get the contract for their aerial spraying I'm sure that alone would drum up custom for me, and the contract itself would be a big one.'

'Why don't you go and see Grevil Robertson?' Kate suggested. 'He's very reasonable. If you like, I'll mention your name to him.'

'Would you, Kate?'

'Of course. Not that I have any say about who they use on my property now, but if I did it would be you for sure. They might be tied up already but there's no harm in mentioning it, I shouldn't think.'

'You're a brick, Kate,' he said warmly.

She laughed. And as they were parting, she said, 'You must come over and see me now you're back, Jim. You won't recognise the twins, they've grown so much.'

'I'd like that very much. You know, *you* don't look a day older!'

'Ah, Jim,' she said ruefully, 'you've made my day, but I think you're stretching the truth a bit!'

Two days later she drove to Cambooya to see Mary Lucas.

After Kate's mother had died, Mary had come in twice a week for years to housekeep for them and Kate had made a practice of keeping in touch with her ever since. She lived now with her son and daughter-in-law at Cambooya, a small nearby hamlet.

But Kate came away feeling depressed because Mary, so bright and vigorous for so long, was obviously failing now and, with the best will in the world, her family were finding her something of a burden.

On the way home, through the stillness of a sunny early afternoon, she came across a broken-down van and stopped to offer assistance. It was a deserted country road and she knew from experience that it could be hours before the next vehicle came along.

Not very long after she'd stopped, however, she began to regret being such a good Samaritan. The driver was a man she knew slightly, and disliked. He had a farm equipment and spare part agency in Pittsworth and was one of those men who was peculiarly unpleasant to deal with—if you were a woman. He also had a wife and four children, by all accounts.

'Well, well!' he said, emerging from beneath the bonnet as she walked up, 'if it isn't Mrs Wiley, our beautiful widow lady!'

Kate regarded him steadily for a moment, caught a whiff of his beer-laden breath and decided he'd probably had a liquid lunch before breaking down. She said abruptly, 'Do you need help or are you just whiling away the time here?'

He laughed. 'I could always do with the kind of help you could give a fella, Mrs Wiley, but it so happens I've got other problems, too, like a blocked fuel line.'

'Then if you'll give me the name of your garage,' Kate said icily, 'I'll ring them when I get home and get them to send someone out for you.' She moved back a couple of paces and couldn't prevent the expression of distaste that crossed her face as more beery fumes floated repulsively down wind.

Norman Farraday narrowed his eyes and followed her and she stepped back again only to find herself up against the side of the van. 'Oh,' he said softly, 'you're a haughty one aren't you, Kate Wiley? That's right, isn't it? Kate? I've heard people talk about you lately. Got a big opinion of yourself, some people say. But then I didn't need anyone to tell me that—I saw it the couple of times you came into the agency. Didn't want to have anything to do with the likes of me though, did you now?'

'No,' Kate said through gritted teeth. 'And I still don't, so will you please get out of my way?'

'All in good time, sweetheart,' he said softly. 'Know what I think? I think you've been a widow for too long now.' He put out a hand to grasp her around the waist and laughed unpleasantly as she flinched. 'Know what I mean?' he said then.

'No,' said Kate steadily, although she did and felt sick to the stomach; she also felt a flicker of fear.

'No?' he said ingenuously and looked her up and down, a slow insolent look that spoke volumes—and kindled within her a spark of fury along with the fear and disgust. 'Oh come on, Katie, admit it,' he said with a grin, his hand moving up towards her breasts, 'you must be panting for a man after so long.'

Kate brought her knee up sharply and had the satisfaction of hearing his breath leave his body in a whistling gasp as he doubled up painfully.

'You low-down *creep*,' she whispered, but tripped as she moved round him to get to the ute. Fortunately, he was still somewhat inconvenienced so she made it to the truck and was able to get in and lock herself in before he was able to straighten up. She turned the key and revved the engine, but Norman Farraday had more or less recovered as she prepared to let out the clutch. He was walking directly towards the ute now and although she couldn't hear what he was saying, she could guess it; his expression was murderous.

She let the clutch out and started to drive the truck straight at him. He stopped walking and taunted her with obscene gestures. Kate hesitated for a fraction of a second, then pushed the accelerator down hard.

How he got out of the way in time, she never knew. And for a few moments, she found it quite amusing watching his antics in the rear-view mirror; he had fallen but he got up sprightly enough and was dancing with rage and brandishing both fists at her. Then it dawned on her that she could have killed him—she'd been angry enough to drive the truck straight at him—and she felt a cold sweat break out on her brow.

She was still suffering from reaction when she got home a few minutes later and it didn't help, when she breasted the hill up the drive from the gate to the house, to see the maroon Range Rover parked beside the garden gate. Grevil Robertson was leaning on the bonnet.

She waved reluctantly, parked the truck in the shed and went back to meet him.

'I was just wondering if you were down in the paddocks,' he said.

'No. No,' she answered and wiped a hand down the side of her blue denim skirt, only to wince and hold it palm up and then glance exasperatedly at the streak of blood on her skirt.

'What's this?' he asked, taking her hand in his.

'I . . . I didn't notice it before but I must have grazed it.'

'How?'

'I . . . tripped,' she said and shivered. 'Yes. I put my hand down to save myself. It's nothing!' she added and tried to pull away, but he wouldn't release her.

'That's a pity,' he murmured and looked up. 'These honourably scarred hands were beginning to look good. Why did you trip, Kate?'

'I don't know,' she said vaguely. 'Did you want to see me about something?'

'Kate, tell me.'

She sighed ostentatiously and looked around. 'There's nothing to tell,' she tried to say patiently. 'I tripped, that's all.'

'And that's why you're looking pale and all shaken up and you're breathing unsteadily. Did you trip down a mountainside?' he queried ironically.

'*No.*' Her grey eyes glittered with a flash of anger but he remained unmoved, still holding her hand.

'I'm not letting you go until you tell me,' he said mildly and with an answering gleam in his eyes— but of amusement. And somehow or other, not long afterwards, she found herself sitting at her own kitchen table, drinking sweet hot tea which he had made, and telling him what had happened—at least, outlining the situation and trying not to go into too many details, a forlorn attempt, though.

'What did he actually say to you?'

'I . . . I wouldn't like to repeat it,' she muttered.

'That bad? So what happened then?'

'I took some action,' she muttered.

'Tell me.'

She sighed. And told him.

He grinned. 'I always knew you were a resourceful lady, Mrs Wiley. Go on.'

But Kate was staring at him indignantly now. 'It's not funny. Nor am I proud of having to do that to anyone.'

He looked at her more soberly. 'It was the best thing you could have done, Kate. He might think twice in future about importuning unwilling females.'

'Widows,' she said tartly, then bit her lip.

'Ah,' Grevil said quietly and with a long, direct look. 'So there was a personal element to it? Kate?' he said when she wouldn't reply.

She said bitterly at last, 'There shouldn't have been. I barely know him and vice versa. But he obviously knows more about . . . ' She stopped abruptly and stood up restlessly. 'I mean,' she went on lamely, 'he's . . . Well, he's once of those awful men who think they're God's gift to women.'

Grevil was silent and when she turned to look at him warily, his hazel eyes were narrowed thoughtfully.

'So then . . . ' She took a breath and launched into the rest of the sordid details she'd been so reluctant to divulge previously, finishing up on a descending scale and genuinely shaken again by the memory of it. 'I could have killed him. I think that's what I wanted to do,' she whispered.

She turned away to surreptitiously mop up a tear, and heard him say, 'Oh, Kate, what am I going to do about you?'

She tensed and swung back. 'What do you mean?'

He stood up.

'If you mean I over-reacted, I know that,' she said hoarsely. 'You can't go around running people down.'

'I didn't mean that and I don't believe you would have anyway,' he interrupted. 'You'd have swerved

in time if you'd had to. I meant that you're very
gallant and spirited but it's a long, lonely road and
I just sometimes wish there was some way I could
help.'

'You have . . . but you have,' she stammered.

'And complicated your life very much in the
process,' he said drily.

She stared at him and a warm, slow tide of colour
crept into her cheeks because she knew what he
meant. But more than that; he was standing only a
foot away from her, looking at her compassion-
ately, and she would have given anything to be able
to take brief respite from what he'd called the long,
lonely road, in his arms . . .

Her lips quivered suddenly and tears beaded her
lashes, but she said huskily, 'I'll be fine, honestly.'

He smiled slightly and reached out to cup her face
and smooth the tears from her lashes with his
thumbs.

She trembled inwardly and valiantly fought the
desire to turn her lips into his palms, to kiss them.
She closed her eyes unhappily and said in a cracked,
unsteady voice, 'Please, I think you'd better go.'

'I can't, not like this,' he said, barely audibly. 'The
fact is, you touch something in me, Kate,' he added,
drawing her into his arms. 'I hate to see you like
this.'

Kate sighed and laid her head on his shoulder,
knowing she shouldn't but thinking—just for a
moment, a moment in time. 'I hate to be like this,'
she whispered. 'I'm better than this usually.'

'You told me that once before.'

She stirred. 'I'm not surprised you don't believe
it.'

'But I do. That's what makes it so hard,' he said quietly and lifted a hand to fiddle with her hair.

Kate stood quite still for a moment, leaning against him and feeling the trembling of sudden longing deep within her. She caught her breath and pushed herself away resolutely.

'No. Grevil, you mustn't even think that—if that's what you're thinking,' she whispered, colouring and dying a little inside at what she saw in his eyes: a spark of something concerned and very personal. For which I have to take full responsibility, she thought desperately. Because I can't hide what he does to me.

'Kate . . . '

'Grevil, it's only pity, this,' she said shakily. 'Don't you see? And I would hate the thought of that apart from all the other complications.' She swallowed.

He said meditatively, 'Do you really think so?'

'Yes! And you must know it. I think I remind you of yourself—that's what it is.'

He stared at her for a long time, his eyes narrowed, until she turned away, no longer able to bear his scrutiny and sick at heart at what she had awoken.

'I think you'd better go,' she said again jerkily.

'And I think I ought to stay,' he replied quietly. 'We can't just ignore this. Don't you think we should discuss it?'

'There's nothing to discuss,' she said tonelessly. 'Nothing I want to discuss anyway,' she added flatly.

'You sound very dictatorial all of a sudden, Mrs Wiley,' he remarked with a tinge of sarcasm.

Kate compressed her lips and swung back to face him suddenly, her grey eyes glinting angrily. 'All right!' she said, 'Let's discuss it. You're engaged to be married. I'm a possibly frustrated widow with a bit of a crush on you and because we happen to live almost next door to each other and because I happen to have an unfortunate propensity for getting myself into trouble, and you for being on hand, we're seeing a lot more of each other than we should be. Which is making things very hard for me, I have to admit, but I think I told you that once before!' She eyed him fiercely and defiantly.

'Go on,' he murmured, watching her with a detached sort of interest which infuriated her, she found.

'What else is there to say?' she flashed, adding ironically, 'Well, you're not a block of wood, are you? I suppose most men would think it a pity not to take advantage of such an opportunity.'

She stopped abruptly because she had seen Grevil Robertson angry before and knew the signs. And in her heart of hearts, she knew she was to blame for what followed, that it had been a horrible thing to say and not what she really believed, but said it she had and now she was going to pay.

'How right you are, Kate,' he drawled, his mouth hardening and his hazel eyes glittering with an angry menace that chilled her to the core. 'Why should I let an opportunity like this go *begging?*'

She gasped at the deliberate insult and moved fearfully but he was too quick for her. She couldn't evade his arms and had absolutely no answer for his strength. What was worse, when his lips sought hers she really panicked and pleaded with him to let her go.

'Oh, no,' he said, raising his head briefly. 'And don't look like a frightened virgin, Kate,' he added. 'I'm sure I don't have to show *you* how to do it.'

'Grevil,' she panted, 'please . . . '

'All right,' he shrugged, 'if that's how you want it,'—he shot her a look of supreme irony from beneath half-closed lids—'so be it.'

His arms loosened about her and she almost cried with relief, but it was to be very short-lived because in the next instant she realised he had no intention of letting her go, he was simply delaying the inevitable—pulling her slowly but inexorably closer, defying her efforts to break free quite gently, and occasionally with a tolerant little smile twisting his lips, and all the time cradling her body in his arms when she rested briefly as he carefully watched her hot, tormented face.

She stopped fighting abruptly, her breasts heaving and her eyes dark.

He waited until some of the colour had left her cheeks and her breathing had steadied, then he said quietly, 'Let me tell you what it would be like, Kate. In case you've forgotten after so long. I could always start with those long, long legs of yours. I could slide your skirt up and touch your thighs. But then again . . . ' He moved her a little away and looked down at the swell of her breasts beneath the cherry cotton of the shirt she wore and his eyes lingered on the V-neck of the shirt and the shadows it revealed, the smooth hollows at the base of her throat. 'I'm sure your breasts are lovely and pale and full and enough to tempt any man—they have a way of moving when you move that promises so much. But perhaps you have your own preference for the order of things. Perhaps you like to start like this.' He bent his head and claimed her lips. And, to her despair, Kate closed her eyes and surrendered with a husky little moan.

But her torment was not quite over, she realised, when he lifted his head at last and she swayed in his arms and could only stare up at him with her lips parted.

'Why yes,' he drawled very softly, 'a good way to begin, it seems. Shall we go on? Something tells me you're a good lover, Kate, that you put your heart and soul into it—as you do most things. Do you like to make love until you're exhausted and that lovely body glistens with sweat? Do you like to touch your partner as well as to be touched? Tell me how you like it, Kate.'

Kate stared up at him and trembled against the strong, hard length of his body as the images his words had created filled her mind and she pictured herself bending over him and trailing her lips across the skin of his wide shoulders. A tide of tell-tale colour crept into her cheeks, and, beneath the thin cotton of her shirt and bra, her nipples hardened.

But he said then, with his hazel eyes mocking her, 'What's this? No fight left in you, Kate? I thought you were better than that. Or perhaps I was right in the first place—you do need a man. What's your considered opinion now, Mrs Wiley? Should I go or should I stay?'

She gasped, but this raking, merciless gaze didn't flicker. 'Oh . . . ' she breathed, and wrenched herself free. 'You *are* no better than the rest of them. I might have known!'

'But you did know,' he said grimly, and deftly caught her hand as she raised it to hit him. 'You had me all worked out—you told me so just now. No different from most men. You know everything, Kate, don't you?' he taunted.

'I . . . Let me go,' she wept, as his hand threatened to crush the bones of her wrist. 'And get out of here and don't ever come back!' she panted.

He released her wrist and laughed. 'Let me know if you change your mind,' he said leisurely and walked out, leaving Kate stunned, and, a few moments later, so angry that she grabbed a beloved plate off the dresser and flung it to the floor.

She discovered over the next few days that her considered opinions were many and varied. She hated Grevil Robertson but then she hated herself, too, for saying what she had, although in the long run hadn't it proved a point? Several, you say, Kate? That you can be a real bitch sometimes— well, but it *is* an impossible situation and I didn't say anything that wasn't true, except, maybe, for the last bit. And that was said in the heat of the moment after a nasty experience which was still rankling—didn't he realise that? Did he have to make his point like a steamroller pinning a butterfly?

Oh, Jenny, she thought, too, I wonder if you know what you're getting yourself into? Have you any idea how damning and dangerous he can be? Isn't it like mating a lamb to a sleeping tiger? Or will love make the difference? she mused ironically.

And there was another thought to plague her, she discovered. What had he meant about complicating her life? Just the obvious or did he have an inkling of what was being said around the district as well? The first time she thought it, she went dead still as a cold, bubbling spring of fear welled up within her. 'Oh, no. Please no,' she whispered. 'I'd hate that.'

Then she found herself wondering about something else, and was amazed that she should care. What had he meant about not having to teach *her* how to do it? To kiss? Well, obviously Jennifer Kent is a very innocent girl—you'd already decided that, Kate. That's what he meant. Why does it bother you, especially now you've decided you hate the man? Or have you?

The net result of her anger and hurt and confusion was something rather dangerous, she discovered. A feeling of wildness, a feeling of—— If there was a war to go to, she'd go, just for the hell of it; a desire to break out although she didn't know how—thank God, she thought ruefully.

She did wage one small war though: on the tennis court. Although repaired, it still needed rolling and painting and tending.

'You'll kill yourself, missus,' Ted Jenkins, the pensioner she'd employed to help her with the garden, said to her after a session with the roller when she came off the court panting and sweating and scarlet in the face. 'Why don't you leave it to me?'

'Oh, I'm as tough as old boots, Ted! Anyway you've got enough to do.'

'Well, I was just saying to Mrs Jenkins the other day that I take my hat off to you, I really do. You can turn your hand to most men's work and do it better than a lot, but I guess it's only old codgers like me who appreciate it.'

Kate raised an eyebrow laughingly. 'What are you trying to say, Ted?'

He leant on his fork and considered. 'That you're only young and pretty once, I guess. And it's a pity to work yourself to death while you are. Why don't you forget the tennis court and go out and give some guy a run for his money?'

'Kate! Are you getting thin again?' Marcie demanded about two weeks after Kate had nearly run a man down and in turn been spiritually, not to mention physically, demolished by Grevil Robertson.

'No, I don't think so,' Kate said.

'What have you been doing then?'

'Well, this and that . . . '

'I thought you were paying people to do this and that for you!'

'I am. I am! But I can't sit around and twiddle my thumbs all day.'

'I can imagine,' Marcie said grimly. 'There's something not quite right with you, Kate Wiley.'

'You're right, Marcie,' Kate murmured, but added hastily, 'There's nothing wrong with me; I was only joking.'

Marcie was silent for a time. They were sitting on the floor of her living-room sorting through a mountain of articles—dolls' clothes, aprons, covered coat-hangers, lavender bags, oven mitts and so on—all made by the mothers of the district and due to go on sale at the forthcoming school fête. Then she said abruptly. 'I've seen you like this twice before, Kate. After Mike died and not so long ago when you sat down and cried and told me life didn't have much meaning for you. It was just after Grevil Robertson had leased your river flats—do you remember? I had hoped things had changed?'

'They have,' Kate said. 'Of course they have!' She smiled. 'I promise you there's not a tear left in me.'

Marcia looked at her sharply. 'I don't like the sound of that!'

Kate shrugged.

'You're not going to tell me this time, are you, Kate?' Marcie looked at her searchingly.

Kate dropped an embroidered doily into her lap and reached for the two smaller ones that made up a matching duchess set. 'There's nothing to tell,' she said quietly. 'How much do you think we should charge for these?'

A fleeting look of hurt crossed Marcie's face, and seeing it, Kate closed her eyes. 'Please,' she whispered, 'there's no point in talking about it. But thanks all the same for being the best friend I ever had.'

'Oh, Kate,' Marcie breathed, watching Kate's fingers clenching and unclenching about the unfortunate doilies. 'I think I might know anyway.' She broke off and bit her lip.

Kate's lashes flew up and her eyes were suddenly wide and fearful.

'Not from anything you . . . I mean . . . ' A flood of colour entered Marcie's cheeks.

'Go on,' Kate said and discovered her mouth was curiously dry.

Marcie bent her head briefly and when she looked up there was still a tinge of colour in her cheeks but a look of decision in her green eyes. 'I have to go on now, don't I? It's Grevil Robertson, isn't it?

'How did you know?'

'It was May originally, although—I don't know why, but I just had a feeling.'

'You told me once not to play with fire.'

'Yes,' Marcie said musingly. 'Not that I believed a word of *May's* gossip,' she added scathingly. 'But at the sports and the tennis party, I could see you were upset about something. Oh, I don't think anyone else noticed but they don't know you as well as I do. And it made me stop and think. I'm *sorry, Kate*,' she said passionately. 'It's just that I hate to see you . . . But I might be quite wrong?'

A shudder went through Kate. 'No. Marcie, will you tell me what May Watson's got against me?'

'I don't know. Perhaps it isn't anything. You know what May's like. If I didn't know Les, I'd say she was a frustrated woman, but he looks like a very red-blooded male to me. Yet sometimes her gossip is pure poison.'

'Neither of them like me,' Kate said shakily, 'but May has never before . . . ' She shrugged helplessly. 'And the stupid part is, the gossip she's spreading is based on something quite innocent. Only, in essence, she's hit the nail on the head.'

'It isn't only May any more,' Marcie said unhappily. 'It's distilled through *like* a kind of poison.'

'I know,' Kate whispered, and told Marcie what had happened with Norman Farraday. Marcie was horrified.

'Kate, you poor thing!'

Kate grimaced. 'What . . . what is May saying?'

Marcie sighed and looked down at her hands. 'That Kate Wiley has come a-cropper, which is no less than she deserves. That Kate has . . . '

'No less than I deserve! What on earth does she mean? Go on.'

'That anyone who breaks up families . . . Kate,' Marcie said helplessly, 'I don't know what she's on about either. But for some reason she's a bitter enemy of yours and she doesn't care who knows it now.'

'Because I can beat her at tennis?' Kate asked dazedly.

'I doubt it. It mightn't have helped, but surely not.'

'There's nothing else! Well, Mike didn't get on very well with Les and neither have I——No, it's less than that, Marcie. I don't like Les but I've never even said as much to anyone but Mike and you.'

'Les Watson isn't an easy man to get on with anyway, Kate. He's bombastic, self-righteous and has quite a few enemies, me included. I got stuck right into him one night at a Parents and Children meeting. May might have been a little cool for a while afterwards but she certainly didn't mount a vendetta like this against me.'

Kate shook her head. 'Then I just don't understand,' she said and added after a while, 'So the whole district now thinks I'm pining for Grevil

Robertson and would like to break up his forthcoming marriage?'

Marcie was silent.

'They are right and wrong, in that order,' Kate
said. 'And,' she added with a bitter but determined
glint in her eyes. 'if it's the last thing I do, I'll prove
to them they were never right at all.'

'Kate, should you . . . I mean, what . . . '

'Marcie, this thing has got to be stopped. Do you
know May has even got Stanley mentioning it to
Serena? God knows, I'm not enjoying it and I
shudder to think what the Robertsons would think
if they knew, but *that* I cannot live with.'

'But how can you prove anything?'

'Believe me, I'll think of a way,' Kate said grimly,
and resolutely ignored the look of concern in her
friend's eyes.

She didn't realise that she wouldn't have to look
very far.

CHAPTER SEVEN

JIM COMPTON turned up at Kunnunurra the next day.

Kate was delighted to see him, then consumed with guilt. 'Oh, Jim,' she said awkwardly after greeting him, 'I—I haven't seen Grevil Robertson yet.'

'That's all right,' he interrupted with a smile. 'I didn't come to see you about that anyway. I came to renew my acquaintance with Matt and Serena, to look the old place over and ask you if you'd care to come to a social evening with me.'

'Where?'

'Dalby. It's some sort of charity hop I promised to attend this Saturday. Anything on?'

'No,' Kate confessed ruefully. 'Thank you, I'd like that. Now sit down and tell me how business is going. Matt and Serena will be home soon.'

Kate enjoyed herself at the Dalby 'hop' but it was only afterwards that it dawned on her how fortuitous it was to have Jim about.

The next weekend she invited him to the mixed tennis party. The Watsons were there and, at the sight of them, Kate was consumed with a desire to have the whole matter out with May Watson—not in public though. She knew she'd be wasting her time, and, anyway, how good would she be at denying the truth? So she had to content herself with some surprised looks and the knowledge that some people would be reviewing the gossip about Kate Wiley now that she had a good-looking, unattached escort.

Yet all the time, she felt a niggle of guilt within.

In a bid to assuage it, she took hold of an opportunity to speak to Stan Ellis at least, when she happened to bump into him in Pittsworth one day.

'Howdy do, Mrs Wiley, the best lady tractor driver this side of the black stump!' Stan said humorously.

'Hello, Stan,' she said with a grin. 'I . . . I haven't seen anyone from Eton for ages. Apart from Tom.'

'Lots of comings and goings,' Stan said rolling his eyeballs. 'They seem to be taking it in turns, Grevil and old Mrs Robertson. But the wedding's only about six weeks off,' he named a date, 'so I guess it's understandable.'

'Yes,' Kate said slowly. 'In Sydney?'

'The wedding? Yep. Miss Kent's father is still in hospital down there, although he's due out soon, but I guess it's best to take it to him. Must say, the sooner the better, I reckon. Long engagements are a bit tough on a bloke and Grevil's starting to show signs of it.' He winked at Kate.

'Stan,' she said a little breathlessly, 'can I ask you something?'

'Fire away!'

'Have you tied up your aerial spraying contract yet?'

'Nope, as a matter of fact we haven't. We took over the previous owner's contract and it comes up for renewal soon but I'm told the firm is folding. Why do you ask?'

She told him. 'Not that either he or I would expect you to deliver the death blow if they're in trouble, this other firm, but as I said, he was a friend of my husband . . . ' She broke off suddenly and looked awkward.

Stan appeared not to notice. 'Tell you what, get him to come and see me. Of course, Grevil's got the final say but if he can deliver the goods, I can recommend him, your friend.'

Kate thanked him sincerely and they parted, but afterwards she stopped to wonder if she hadn't done Jim's cause more harm than good. If Grevil knew who had recommended him in the first place . . . Oh, hell, why don't I stop to think? she chastised herself. But of other things, she promptly refused to allow herself to think at all.

Jim was very grateful when she mentioned the matter to him, however, but she said,

'Jim, look, I must warn you it might not come to anything. Stan said himself that Grevil has the final say.'

'Fair enough,' Jim said easily. 'But you told me yourself he's a reasonable sort of guy and he's done the right thing by you.'

She hesitated, 'Well, yes, but that was a bit different. I don't think I told you that Mike saved his life once.'

Jim eyed her and she knew immediately that she was tying herself up in knots and that he was curious to know why. But all he said was, 'Getting married soon, isn't he?'

'Yes. By the way, the local P & C are having their annual dinner in Toowoomba and Marcie Hunter is bulldozing me into going. I haven't been to one since Mike died but, well, I wondered if . . . ' she paused briefly, 'if you'd like to come with me.'

'I'd love to, Kate,' he said warmly.

Kate turned away and thought, Oh God, I'm only using Jim. I forgot all about him after we met that day in Toowoomba but when he turned up here, it was like manna from heaven, grist to the mill of my plan to prove to everyone that I'm not in love with Grevil Robertson . . . What have you *become,* Kate?

'Something wrong, Kate?' Jim said quietly from behind her.

She turned and smiled up at him. 'No! I . . . I . . . How's business otherwise?'

'You asked me that half an hour ago,' he said, his eyes resting on her thoughtfully. She'd forgotten that very little escaped those blue eyes.

He waited and she tried to speak but couldn't. Then he took her hand and said quietly, 'If something's troubling you, Kate, if there's something you'd like to tell me, I wish you would. But if it's hard to talk about, don't feel you have to explain anything to me. I enjoy your company but I'd never take advantage of it. So if you're,' he paused and looked at her very directly, 'rather needing some kind of moral support at the moment, I'm perfectly happy to be it with no strings attached.'

'How did you know?' she whispered.

'I didn't. It was an educated guess.'

'You're very kind,' she said, her grey eyes shimmering with tears.

'Not at all,' he replied with a grin. 'Anyway, it's good for business to be mixing with the locals so if you've any more dinners or whatevers up your sleeve . . . '

'Oh, Jim . . . '

In the end, though, he couldn't make it.

He rang Kate on the Friday morning—the dinner was that evening—and he was both excited and full of apologies. Excited because he had got the Eton contract . . .

'You did?' Kate said disbelievingly into the phone.

'Yes! They've just contacted me and that's why I feel all the more guilty about letting you down tonight, Kate. I owe it all to you but the fact is, the crop duster I'm buying has become available sooner than I expected. I can fly down to Brisbane today on a commercial flight and fly it back tomorrow. Now that gives me a few extra days in hand for any modifications it might need——'

'Jim, I understand,' she interrupted, 'really I do. Business comes first, especially at this crucial stage. Come and see me when you get the chance.'

'You're a brick, Kate!'

She put the phone down and then rang Marcie to tell her they would be one short tonight; also to test the water, in a manner of speaking, as to Marcie's reaction should they become two short.

'But you're still coming, aren't you, Kate?' Marcie said immediately down the line.

'Well . . . '

'Oh, Kate, you must come. Think of your new dress. And I swear to God no one will treat you like a wallflower or a predatory widow or a . . . '

'Marcie,' Kate said laughingly, 'don't go on. Um . . . '

'Yes, the Watsons will be there, Kate,' Marcie said firmly, 'so you'll just have to be brave about that. But no, so far as we know, Grevil Robertson will not.'

'So far as you know?'

'Well, you know it's our policy to invite all the parents whether they're on the P & C or not, so I did ring him but he said he thought he would be away and would have to take a raincheck. He was very nice about it, actually. Quite sounded as if he found the doings of the P & C of interest.'

'Well . . . ' Kate said.

'Now let me think, you'll need a lift. What time are you dropping the kids off at the Jenkins?'

'Ted is coming to pick them up at five-thirty,' Kate said weakly.

'Excellent! Roy and I will pick you up at six-thirty. Make it six-fifteen. That means we'll be in town by seven-thirty with no problems. Now, remember that face mask I used to make you?'

'Marcie . . . '

'Make yourself one this afternoon. It's marvellously relaxing as well as everything else. See you later, Kate!'

Kate put the phone down slowly and stood staring at it. Then she shrugged and squared her shoulders ruefully.

She saw the children off at five-thirty. They were spending the night with the Jenkins, and were quite excited because Ted Jenkins, Matt had discovered, was a miniature train enthusiast. Mrs Jenkins had sent a message to Kate via Ted to tell her to have 'a real good sleep in' before worrying about picking the children up the next morning.

She waved them off and wandered inside to get dressed. She had taken Marcie's advice—God knows why, she thought wryly—but felt better for it. She had also showered, done her nails, washed her hair and dried it and even put her dress on for Serena, who had wanted to see how she would look. Then taken it off.

She stared down at it now, lying on her bed. She and Marcie had chosen it together and it was like nothing she had worn for years. A pale, rose-pink chiffon with big shadowy green flowers, it had a simple straight bodice with a round neck and no sleeves and a lowered waistline with a full, gathered skirt. And around the dropped waistline, a brighter pink, shirred taffeta sash.

'Oh,' Kate had said to her reflection in the mirror in the shop. 'Oh, I don't know . . . '

'Oh, but I do!' Marcie's green eyes had sparkled. 'Kate, it's gorgeous! It's feminine, you have the figure and the height to carry it off . . . '

'And it's the only one of its kind on the Downs,' the saleslady had murmured. 'I also happened to notice a pair of shoes, the identical pink, in the shop next door. And we have this lovely little ivory angora jacket that would go over it perfectly. See, it has short gathered sleeves and these silver sequins round the neck—very delicate!'

'Won't it be too dressy, though?' Kate had asked Marcie anxiously.

'Darling, you haven't been to our dinner for the last four years so you probably don't remember that we go the whole hog: strapless, backless, laces and taffetas. No, it won't be too dressy but it will be classy. You'll be the envy of all of us.'

'I don't know if that sounds a very good idea, with my record,' Kate had said wryly. 'On the other hand . . .'

'Precisely! Buy it,' Marcie had ordered.

Dear Marcie, Kate mused, coming out of her reverie, you seem to have to be chivvying me along a lot these days.

She sighed and presently got dressed.

She used make-up sparingly because her skin was really looking good now; she had used a blow dryer on her hair so that it had lift and body and she wore it loose to her shoulders. Her father had given her a string of seed pearls for her eighteenth birthday and she wore those, together with Mike's wedding present, a pair of cultured pearl earrings. That was all. She dabbed some Shalimar cologne behind her ears and on her pulse spots—an absolutely wicked extravagance on her part, but, as a confidence booster when worn with this dress, somehow unique and worth every cent.

Then she heard a toot outside, and she realised with a start how the time had flown. As she reached for her angora jacket and swung it off the bed, she caught a glimpse of herself in the mirror, with her hair swinging out and her skirt belling and for an instant it was Kate from another era—tall, lithe, attractive, vital . . .

She stopped dead still and considered this image. Her eyes were a clear luminous grey but . . . Ah, that's the difference, she thought. I can emulate *that* Kate on the outside but will the inner me ever feel as vital and carefree and confident again?

Marcie was a little quiet on the way in, Kate thought. But she had said that Pete had been reluctant to go his babysitter for some reason she couldn't fathom, so Kate attributed it to this.

Not long after the party, thirty or so strong, had assembled in the bar area of the restaurant for pre-dinner drinks, Kate was forced to revise her opinions, because, to most people's surprise and Kate's horror, Grevil Robertson was the last to arrive.

She saw him enter the restaurant, wearing a conservative dark suit and white shirt; she saw him hesitate and glance around; then she saw Marcie . . . *Marcie,* walk over to claim him with a welcoming smile and lead him back to the bar to start introducing him all round.

Before they got to Kate, Roy took over the introductions and Marcie slipped to Kate's side, 'Don't hate me, Kate, please!' she whispered out of the corner of her mouth.

'I . . . Did you know all the time?'

'*No.* He rang me this afternoon and said he'd just remembered the dinner and as he wasn't away after all, was there any possibility at this late stage of him coming! What could I *say?*'

'You could have warned me, at least.'

'You would have backed out!'

'I . . . It's what I should have done in the first place,' said Kate bitterly.

'Kate, you can't avoid him for ever. Oh, Kate, you can handle this, I know you can. They're coming this way.' She broke off and smiled up at

Grevil Robertson. 'Roy doesn't have to introduce you to Kate, does he?'

Kate looked up, with her heart suddenly pounding and her mouth dry, and was instantly aware of May Watson, resplendent in turquoise taffeta, hovering as if irresistibly drawn.

'No. How are you, Kate?' Grevil said easily and with a smile. 'My grandmother sends her regards and says she's sorry not to have seen you lately but she's been in Sydney most of the time, and Jenny sends her love.'

If Kate opened her mouth but was unable to speak for a moment, May Watson's jaw literally sagged.

Marcie dug Kate in the ribs surreptitiously and Kate responded, although she had no idea what she said. But it must have been all right because moments later she and Marcie and Roy and Grevil were engaged in a light-hearted conversation, and that Grevil Robertson and Kate Wiley shared a peculiarly tortured relationship would not have entered any spectator's head.

Why? Kate wondered dazedly and was to wonder it again and again throughout the evening. Why is he doing it? I thought we hated each other. I thought I gave him cause to despise me. I just don't understand; there's something strange going on.

She ate asparagus sitting opposite him at a table for eight. Fortunately, they ate by candlelight so every expression didn't have to be carefully censored.

She ate grilled sole for the main course, and listened to Grevil recounting to the table how Mike had saved his life once.

'So naturally,' he finished, 'the well-being of the Wiley family means a lot to me and I was only too happy to catch up with them again.'

She toyed with a mocha mousse dessert and marvelled at what he'd done—achieved something of long standing between the two of them without actually saying so and without actually lying, and attached a respectability to it, what's more. Oh, she thought suddenly, and pushed her dessert away unfinished, I think I begin to see. He's heard the gossip. If he hadn't before, he has now, and this is a calculated plan to scotch it. How clever, and I wonder if Marcie didn't have something to do with it? I bet she did.

She looked up and straight into those hazel eyes over the candle flame, to see that for the moment all the casual friendliness was gone from them, and that instead there was a direct, cool challenge in them as if he was saying, you've got a part to play, too, Mrs Wiley.

It occurred to her briefly to wonder who had complicated whose life the more, and she shivered inwardly to think how angry he'd be at the thought of bringing Jenny back to the gossip and the rumours.

She looked away and gathered herself with an effort . . . She was not to know that May Watson, who rarely drank, was making an exception this evening for reasons of her very own that had nothing to do with Grevil Robertson.

There was a small dance floor with a band, and after dinner quite a few people drifted on to it. Kate excused herself and bumped into a distracted looking Marcie on the way to the powder room.

'Marcie, I want to ask you . . . ' she began, then said, 'What is it?'

'It's Pete. Appendicitis, so the babysitter thinks. They're bringing him into town and Roy and I are going over to the hospital. I *knew* there was something wrong. I should never have left him. Kate, you'll be all right to get a lift home, won't you?'

'Yes, but can't I come with you—to the hospital?' Kate said anxiously.

'No. No, Roy and I will be fine, but thanks. Anyway it's going so well, isn't it?'

'If you mean what I think you mean, yes,' Kate said.

'Oh, Kate . . . '

'It doesn't matter, Marcie. Don't worry about it.'

'He . . . Kate, to be honest, he rang me this afternoon to find out what exactly was going on. He'd heard something, obviously. So I levelled with him. Well, someone had to do something!' Marcie said rapidly. 'And that's when he said he'd like to come to the dinner tonight.'

'Well, so far, he's done a brilliant job, Marcie,' Kate said with a smile. 'Now listen, off you go and don't even think about it again. And give my love to Pete!'

The floor-length mirror in the powder room reflected Kate's image admirably. Her lovely dress was still lovely and, if she'd had any doubts about it, the admiration she'd seen in most eyes when she had arrived would have confirmed it. In fact, only Les Watson had looked at her without surprise and he had turned abruptly away. Fortunately, the Watsons weren't at Kate's table but the one next door and she stopped to wonder if May wasn't feeling a trifle foolish. Anyone at the next table with a good sense of hearing would have heard the story about Mike saving Grevil Robertson's life. In fact, Kate had got the distinct impression that a lot of people at other tables might have stopped to listen; that story had been a stroke of genius.

Well, May, I can't say I feel too sorry for you, Kate mused, and, taking a deep breath with a feeling akin to girding her loins, she prepared to face the fray again.

But it was Grevil she had to face first.

As she came back to the table it was to see only one couple sitting with him and they got up to dance not long after she arrived.

Remembering that challenging glance, she said lightly, 'There's something I wanted to thank you for.'

He sipped his wine and raised an eyebrow at her.

'For giving your aerial spraying contract to Jim Compton. He was a friend of Mike's . . . ' She ran dry and swallowed.

'You don't have to thank me,' Grevil said after a moment. 'He got it because he was able to demonstrate that he could come up with the goods.'

'I wouldn't have recommended him otherwise,' Kate said tartly, but immediately pinned a false smile to her lips. 'On the other hand it did occur to me that any recommendation coming from me might have damned his cause.' She reached for her own wine glass and raised it in an ironic little toast.

She was rewarded by a gleaming white grin, accompanied by a lazy look, and he murmured, 'Business is business, Kate. By the way, you're looking very lovely tonight. Another new dress?'

She shivered inwardly and, with a sudden, haunting sense of desolation, wished she could read his mind as he sat across from her, his thick fair hair looking tawny gold in the candlelight, his conservative suit not hiding the width of his shoulders but, together with the white shirt and blue tie, emphasising the sophisticated, worldly side of him. The unspoken aura of a man who could probably buy and sell everyone in the restaurant ten times over and run rings round them in most ways, if he chose. But he rarely chose to give full rein to that side of him, she knew; that was why he was so liked. Except, that is, she thought, for me. He chose, last time we met, to . . . do what he did . . . yet now he's sitting there and I don't know what he's really thinking. Is he still angry? Despising me, and maybe even more so now? Oh, God . . .

Before she could answer, some of their companions drifted back from the dance floor and the moment was gone.

She didn't dance and neither did Grevil, and she saw approval in some eyes for these tactics, and reflected wryly that socialising as a widow was like crossing a minefield without a map.

But she did circulate and manage to while away the evening quite pleasantly, even to think that she was going to get through it without making a fool of herself.

So when she was sitting at the table, alone for the moment but content to be so for a while, she was totally unprepared for what was to ensue, when May sat down opposite her and regarded her as steadily as was possible for someone in the first stages of intoxication.

'Hello, May,' she said quietly after a moment.

'Kate,' May said measuredly, 'I've come to tell you something.'

'Oh? What?' Kate asked warily.

'You're a bitch,' May said pleasantly.

Kate's mouth fell open. Then she glanced around but most people were dancing, Les was at the bar deep in conversation and Grevil she couldn't see.

'You're one of those women men can't keep their eyes off,' May went on. 'You're a menace really. There should be a law about the likes of you.'

Kate closed her eyes and tried to count to ten but that little flame of anger which May's poisonous insinuations had ignited weeks ago whooshed into a flame of fury.

'Are you jealous because you're not quite so successful with men, May?' she asked sweetly. 'Perhaps you should take a leaf out of my book?' She stared at May Watson with cold irony, and not the slightest intimation of what her words were to unleash.

'I only wanted to be succesh . . . successful with one man, Kate,' May said, correcting herself carefully, 'but I'd die rather than take a leaf out of your book.'

'What . . . what are you talking about?' Kate whispered.

'Les,' May said and laughed when Kate's eyes widened. 'Don't tell me you didn't know?'

'Know what?' Kate asked with an effort and a sudden blinding and sinking certainty. 'You don't mean . . . ' She licked her lips.

'Oh, but I do!' May said expansively, quite as if this was an ordinary conversation. 'From the moment he laid eyes on you he was . . . what's the word?—smitten; *smitten.* I got that right, didn't I?' She smiled at Kate, then looked anxious. 'Don't think he hasn't hated himself for it, Kate, and you. And I know he would never dream of being unfaithful to me with you, but you see . . . '

Kate watched in mesmerised horror as tears gathered in May's eyes and her lips worked before she went on, 'But you see, ever since I realised it, I've never been able to put it out of my mind; nothing's ever been the same since.'

The words and the tears gathered momentum and Kate sat in stunned, frozen immobility as May poured forth the saga of a marriage turned sour and bitter; of the curious paradoxes it had produced— how they had joined forces to be critical of Kate and how May had relished that even though she had known why Les was doing it; of how he had said Kate's name one night in his sleep, only once, but wasn't that bad enough?

'Stop. Oh, God, stop,' Kate pleaded desperately. 'I didn't even know; I never dreamt; I . . . May, please don't do this to yourself,' she whispered as May's face contorted and she gathered herself. But a voice from behind them interrupted.

It was Les Watson, saying his wife's name sharply.

Kate turned convulsively to see both Les and Grevil standing directly behind them, and worse, that the whole happy party had come to a dead stop and people were staring in embarrassment, but with a fascination that would not let them tear their eyes away.

May Watson looked owlishly up at her husband and said, 'I was just telling Kate why I don't like her, Les. But you know all about it, don't you? Did you know that I did, too? Ever since I saw you watching her once.' And she laid her head down on the table and wept.

The next few minutes were like a nightmare. Les Watson shot Kate a look of such blazing anger and venom that she flinched visibly. Then he half-walked, half-carried May out and everyone started to dance again, but without much enjoyment.

Kate stumbled to her feet and walked out, too, white-faced and trembling.

She stopped on the pavement and saw Les and May turn the corner further down and she stared after them with despair.

Then she felt a hand on her arm; it was Grevil. She looked up at him through a haze of tears and tried to turn and walk away, but he said,

'The Rover's just across the road. Come.'

'I . . . I . . . ' she said dazedly.

'Kate, walk,' he commanded.

She did because she couldn't seem to think straight, couldn't think of anything else to do.

Once in, she started   cry silently.

It was only a short drive he took her on and she realised dimly that they had stopped in a driveway before a large white house—from what she could see by the light of a lone lamp-post on the pavement.

'Where . . . What . . . ' she stammered.

'This was the Morcambes' house,' he said quietly. 'It came in the package deal with Eton. I sometimes spend the night here.' He opened his door and got out and came round to help her.

'But I . . . '

'Just do as you're told, Kate.'

She sobbed once and bit her lip on a rising tide of hysteria. He put his hands around her waist and bodily lifted her down, and he kept his hand on her arm until they were inside.

She looked around as Grevil lit lamps and closed curtains. It was a large lounge, furnished rather heavily and without the grace and beauty of the Eton drawing-room. She caught sight of herself in a huge mirror over the fireplace and stared at her reflection. And hated herself suddenly, despite her red eyes and blotchy cheeks.

'I didn't know,' she said hoarsely. 'I really had no idea!' She wiped her nose on the back of her hand.

'Here,' Grevil said. 'Sit down and drink this.'

He guided her over to a large settee, sat down beside her and handed her a glass of brandy.

She sipped it, her teeth chattering against the rim, and then pushed the glass back at him and dropped her head into her hands.

'Was I blind or what?' she wept in anguish. 'I thought he hated me.'

'Did you honestly never suspect?' Grevil said.

'No! Why should I?' She looked up.

He shrugged.

'Don't you believe me?'

'Yes I do, Kate, but . . . ' He stopped and watched her sombrely.

'But what?'

'Well, it did occur to me.'

'When?' she whispered.

'When you first told me about him, the day your bridge fell into the creek.'

'I don't see how it could possibly have. I . . . '

'Kate, all I thought was that when Les Watson first laid eyes on you, you must have been gorgeous. I just couldn't imagine any man taking a dislike to you on *sight*. And you seemed quite sure there was no other reason.' He smiled slightly. 'So it crossed my mind that perhaps the opposite had occurred.'

'So I was blind—and stupid,' she said bitterly.

'I didn't say that. It often takes an outsider to see these things.'

'Or a wife.'

He was silent for a time, then he said, 'Don't torment yourself because you didn't know, Kate. It wouldn't have helped Les Watson.'

'It might have helped me. And May. You don't know what I said to her.'

'As a matter of fact, I do. I had started to come back to the table before the others.'

Kate winced and pressed her knuckles to her mouth. 'It was a horrible thing to say.'

'She wasn't being exactly complimentary to you,' he said drily and added, 'If it's achieved one thing, it's made things clear to me. Marcie, by the way . . . '

'She told me,' Kate said.

'Well, she didn't mention any names, just that someone who seemed to bear you a grudge had started the whole business and based it on something quite innocent—she said you'd told her that.'

Kate grimaced. 'It was.' She described how May had seen them after the sports. 'Only, of course, the ironical part of it all . . . '

'Kate,' he interrupted, 'don't.'

'No,' she whispered and tried to smile. 'What I can't understand, though, is why she waited so long—May, I mean. Just for the right opportunity, do you think?'

He studied her. 'I doubt it,' he said finally. 'What did it was probably the fact that you were getting back to the old, brilliant, lovely Kate, and she found herself resenting that, I'd say.'

Kate laid her head back wearily. 'I'm only sorry it had to affect you,' she said presently. 'But I thought you handled it marvellously tonight. God knows what people are going to think now, though.'

'They might understand now, as I do,' he said quietly. 'Kate, you could have come to me and told me what you were going through.'

'I . . . ' She swallowed. 'I felt such a fool. The very last thing I wanted was for you to know, especially . . . ' She stopped.

'After our last meeting? I'm sorry about that.'

'I think I asked for it.'

'The man you nearly ran over,' he said, 'did he refer to it?'

'Yes.'

He reached out a hand and picked up one of hers. They sat like that in silence for some minutes then Kate turned her head away and started to cry again. 'It seems such a terrible waste,' she wept. 'All those years of not being able to communicate with each other, all the bitterness that May had locked up in herself . . . Even if she'd come out and confronted him I don't think it could have been worse, because I can't help thinking she sort of helped to build it up out of all proportion.'

'I think you're right, possibly,' he said. 'You know, perhaps she never felt very secure as a wife, in that role. She might have had inhibitions she didn't know how to handle—and had them before you ever arrived on the scene. People react strangely to their insecurities. Sometimes with an inflated sense of,'—he shrugged—'pride. I guess what I'm trying to say is that the seeds of this had to be within May or Les or both. You were just the catalyst.'

Kate shuddered and found that she couldn't stop the tears, that she felt consumed by a sea of sadness and futility.

He said after a while, 'Don't, Kate.'

'I'm sorry, I can't help it. I . . . I . . . ' She rubbed at her eyes furiously and started to cough.

When he moved closer and deliberately took her in his arms, she struggled weakly. 'No! No, you mustn't, Grevil.'

'I know,' he said into her hair, 'but I am.'

She fought for breath then sagged against him. Gradually she calmed down, apart from the odd little hicuppy breath. And finally, she lay with her cheek against his shirt, listening to his heart beating.

'Kate?' he said, and pushed some wet strands of hair off her face.

Her lashes fluttered and she looked up into his eyes, seeing the golden green flecks in the greyness and the curiously intent expression.

She licked her lips. 'Grevil?' she whispered, feeling her pulses beginning to race.

His wandering fingers traced the outline of her mouth then slid into her hair and he bent his head to kiss her.

Oh, God. Oh, no, she thought, I've done it again. But this time she seemed powerless to put up any show of resistance.

The master bedroom of the Morcambe residence which now belonged to Grevil Robertson was just as solidly furnished as the lounge, but it did have a rather lovely, wide, four-poster bed complete with frilled canopy.

Kate stared up at the canopy and closed her eyes and felt herself go hot and cold as she remembered. Grevil was asleep beside her.

Why did I do it? she asked herself. Because he gave me no choice? No, it wasn't like that. It was as if I crossed over a point of no return when he kissed me, as if he was the only spar I had to cling to in that sea of sadness and loneliness. So I didn't say a word when he brought me up here and undressed me. And then . . . and then I crossed another point of no return, a point where desire and aching need fused and I just couldn't go back. But did I have to be so . . . *so* . . .

She bit her lip and blushed in the darkness but nothing could stop her remembering their love-making . . .

Silence . . .

It's so quiet, she thought dimly as she stood in the bedroom, leaning against him because he'd just finished kissing her again, as quiet as Kunnunurra.

Then she felt his hands move up to the back of her neck and felt her dress part as he slid the zip down. She stepped out of it and back into his arms and shivered.

'Cold?' he murmured against the corner of her mouth.

'No.' It was only a breath of sound.

He took her bra off and stared down with fascination at her freed breasts, pale and full and luscious with dark rose nipples, and he traced his fingers around their paler pink areola.

She trembled and watched his fingers and saw her nipples harden. She made a husky little sound in her throat and closed her eyes and brought her hands up to his chest.

'Kate?'

She opened her eyes and stared up into his.

'Come,' he said and picked her up, but only to lay her on the bed and with infinite care, to slide her tights and lacy briefs off. She trembled anew at the feel of his fingers on the soft, inner skin of her thighs, and on her slender ankles, and she sighed when his hands left her body.

He stood up and she watched his every movement in the dim lamplight as he took his clothes off. She waited with her cheek resting on the pillow, her hair splayed out in luxurious abandon, for him to come back to her. But he stood for a moment staring down at her, at the grace of her body, the long legs, the paler ivory skin of her hips and waist and breasts, the glistening triangle of curls below the slight, soft mound of her stomach.

Then he looked at her face and their gazes locked soberly, but it was too late. She raised her arms and he came into them.

She kissed his throat softly and felt his hands roaming at will over her, and she thought her skin had never felt so soft and warm and silken. She kissed his shoulder and his skin was smooth and supple . . . And that's when she lost control, she was to think later.

But it was no longer possible to be contained. Passivity fled her and a yearning kind of joy took its place. She felt transfused, translated, transcendent. She felt so vibrant with love she couldn't be still—she felt like a violin playing sweet and high and taut. She was ecstatic, then grave and intent in turn.

He pulled the pillow up behind him and sat her astride his lap and she gasped then went still as he kissed her breasts, teased her nipples with his teeth, buried his face in their fullness. She cupped the back of his head in her hands and cradled it to her, she slid her hands down the back of his neck as she arched her throat above his head, she cried out softly as his hands moved from her armpits down her back to the curve of her hips, she pressed light, fluttering kisses on his hair and crooned husky, indistinguishable words of love, his name, her joy . . .

And later, their timing was perfect, their climax simultaneous and so moving, it was as if the earth itself had moved for Kate; to her everlasting shame, she buried her teeth in his shoulder before she realised what she was doing and bit the pillow instead.

It seemed like an age before he eased the corner of the pillowslip away and kissed her lips.

'Sorry!' she whispered and felt him smile against her cheek, and murmur,

'You never do anything in half measures, do you, Kate?'

She stiffened, but he held her closer. 'Don't do that. I only meant that you were wonderful.'

'No, you were. I was . . . '

I was . . . like a starving person at a feast? she asked herself, still staring up at the canopy above the bed although she could barely see it in the darkness. I was totally abandoned; yes, I was.

She closed her eyes and sighed.

She had slept in his arms afterwards; for hours, she thought, because the darkness beyond one window of the bedroom where the curtains weren't properly drawn was losing its density, and as she lay there, she heard a rooster crow. She turned over quietly and buried her head in her arms, and couldn't imagine why she felt invaded by a spirit of calm. Or is it only numbness? she wondered. I should be hating myself; I'm sure I will soon. I wouldn't be surprised if all the dark spirits of hell descended on my soul soon. But in the meantime, there's something I have to do, isn't there? A case I have to put . . .

She thought about it as the light grew imperceptibly and Grevil slept beside her. And she trembled with the desire to reach out to him, to slide back into his arms and press herself close to the lean, hard planes of his body.

Instead, she slipped out of the bed quietly and looked around and saw a navy blue robe hanging on the back of the door. It was too big for her; she knew it was his and closed her eyes and buried her face in it for a moment. Then she turned back to the bed guiltily, but he hadn't stirred.

She bent down and picked up her dress and her underclothes and laid them on a chair and did the same for his clothes. Then she moved silently over to the partly opened curtain and looked out with a feeling of a Martian landed on earth because she had no idea where they were. She gasped, because the view from the upper storey of the house was magnificent in the light of dawn. It was perched, she realised, almost on the edge of the Great Dividing Range, facing east, and the Lockyer Valley below unfolded mile after mile towards the Marburg Range and fled into the horizon.

Kate stared, entranced, as the light grew stronger, then thought she heard a sound and turned.

He was awake, lying with his head propped on one arm, watching her. She immediately felt weak with love as she looked into those hazel eyes, and consumed by a need to go over to him and smooth his ruffled hair off his forehead, trace her fingers across the blue shadows along his jaw . . . And she was unable to stop her lips from forming into a trembling little smile. 'Hello,' she said huskily.

For a moment he didn't respond. Then he smiled back and held out his hand to her.

She blinked away a foolish tear, hesitated, then walked over to the bed and put her hand into his. He pulled her down beside him gently but insistently and she curled up on top of the sheet facing him, but as he bent his head to kiss her she touched her fingers to his lips and said softly, 'No. Please, no, and I don't want you to say anything either. I . . . It was . . . Perhaps I don't have to tell you how it was for me.' Her fingers moved down the column of his neck to a faint red mark on his shoulder and she bit her lip and closed her eyes briefly.

'Kate . . . '

'No,' she whispered, and managed to look up at him ruefully. 'Don't. It was what I needed, desperately. I don't think I've ever felt more lonely or . . . alienated and sad as I did last night. And you knew that, didn't you? That's why you did it and perhaps you'll never know how much it . . . helped. But to . . . ' She paused. 'Now to try to dissect it or to feel guilty or to think of ways to justify it can only flaw it for me so I'm not going to. I . . . ' Her voice shook a little but she smiled up at him. 'I'm going to gather strength and confidence from it but for me, for both of us, it's the final chapter, the last page.'

They stared into each other's eyes for an age, he sombrely and intently, she calmly but pleadingly.

Then he said, 'Oh, Kate,' and smoothed her hair and kissed her on the mouth gently, and lay back with a sigh, one hand still fiddling with her hair, the other across his forehead.

And she knew she'd won her case.

A little later he said, 'I can still get you breakfast before I take you home. Is that permitted?'

Her lips curved into a smile as he sat up. 'Oh, definitely.'

CHAPTER EIGHT

SUMMER advanced. Under the warm, sunny skies, the earth bloomed, the days got longer and the flies got worse, but it was all a welcome release from the rigours of winter.

Kate saw quite a lot of Jim Compton and could only be pleased that his business was flourishing. She also saw a lot of Marcie, and Pete recovered splendidly from his appendectomy. The only link she had with Eton was via Tom and even that ceased after a couple of weeks when he went to Sydney.

'Some people have all the luck!' Serena grumbled one day. 'They get weeks and weeks off school just because their father's getting married in Sydney. Why don't you get married to someone in Sydney, Mum?'

Kate smiled faintly.

'Yes, but he's still going to have to do school work,' Matt said. 'He told me that Mrs Robertson makes him do some every day. And anyway, he's the only one.'

'He is not! Look at Stanley Watson . . . '

'I mean,' Matt persisted, 'Tom's the only one whose father is getting married in Sydney. The way you said it, it sounded as if there was a whole bunch of us getting weeks and weeks off school because we've got dads getting married in Sydney!'

Serena stared at her brother haughtily. 'You know what I meant,' she said indignantly. 'And there *are* two of us getting weeks and weeks off school, Tom and Stanley Watson!'

'Well he might have to do school work, too,' Matt said reasonably, and it occurred to Kate that he was a reasonable little boy—sometimes to his sister's annoyance. 'Because,' he went on, 'he's staying with his grandmother while his Mum and Dad are on holiday and she'll probably do the same as Mrs Robertson.'

'It's still not the same as having to go to school every day and . . . '

'Serena,' Kate interrupted, having had much experience of these kind of arguments and their capacity for degenerating into brawls, 'I thought we might have a salad for supper. Would you like to try those radish rosettes and carrot curls, or whatever they're called, that we saw in the recipe book?'

Serena jumped up enthusiastically.

They'd been sitting on the veranda as the warm, scented day drew to a close. Matt followed Serena inside, then reappeared with his cricket ball and wandered off into the garden to practise his bowling. Kate stayed where she was for a time, thinking.

The only person she'd discussed the awful incident at the P & C dinner with, apart from Grevil, had been Marcie. And only because once she had emerged from her urgent maternal responsibilities and stopped blaming herself for leaving Pete that night, Marcie had belatedly sensed that a very awkward aura seemed to be surrounding the evening.

'Why is everyone so sheepish about it?' she demanded of Kate. 'Did something happen after Roy and I left?'

'I'm surprised you haven't heard,' Kate murmured.

'Well, that's just it. No one seems to be game to talk about it. I mean, I know I'm about a week behind the times, but . . . Kate,' she said with sudden urgency, 'it . . . Not . . . It wasn't . . . '

Kate grimaced. 'Yes, it was me, if that's what you're going to say. But not quite the way you might be imagining.'

'Oh, God,' Marcie said after Kate had told her what had happened, 'so *that* was it! I mean what was bugging May. Of course! It all makes sense now.'

'It's a great pity it didn't make sense sooner,' Kate said.

'Yes,' Marcie agreed ruefully. 'But I hope you're not blaming yourself for that,' she added vigorously.

'There are some things I will always blame myself for, Marcie,' Kate said quietly. 'But I can only hope and pray that Les and May will come together again. He's taken her away on holiday, so . . . ' She shrugged and studied her hands. When she looked up it was to see Marcie watching her closely and she took a breath. 'Other than that, I'm trying very hard to regard that whole period as a . . . '— she swallowed as the words seemed to stick in her throat—'as a closed book.'

'Amen,' Marcie said after a long time. 'I think— I do think that's what we all should do. In fact,' she said with some surprise, 'I think that's what happening. People are feeling guilty because we had such a field day of gossip and never really stopped to imagine the consequences, even though May started it all. I think they dearly want for it all to be put to rest now.'

'I hope so,' Kate said. 'It's not going to be easy for May, anyway.'

'Or you.'

'Not quite so hard for me. And I'm tough, you know.'

Tough, she thought, as the sun slipped over the horizon, and closed her eyes. Oh, God, will I ever forget? How to stand the pain, the sense of loss. What to do about the future. Can I bear it here, so close, and yet where else is there any future for me? I have to bear it. And really, it's only when I'm alone or tired sometimes that I think about it. Otherwise . . . yes, the trick is to keep busy.

Kate realised then that Serena was calling her and she stood up with a sigh of relief.

She packed day after day with as much activity as she could, went out to dinner once with Jim and accepted his invitation to go up with him for a joy ride. Serena and Matt went, too, and loved it.

'I know what I'm going to be when I grow up now,' Matt said that night. Jim had come to have supper with them.

'Let me guess,' Kate said with a wink at Jim. 'A fireman?'

'No! A pilot!' Matt said ingenuously.

'Last week it was a racing driver,' Serena murmured but added, 'I wouldn't mind learning to fly a plane either, actually. Is it very hard, Jim?'

'Yes, how does it work? How *do* planes fly, Jim?' Matt asked eagerly. Kate cast Jim a sympathetic look but he took it all in good part. In fact, as Kate washed up, they sat around the table and he drew them diagrams and as she watched the three of them, so absorbed, she thought how well they got along.

Later that night, when Jim left, she accepted his brief kiss and thanked him warmly for a lovely day. And she stood staring down the drive in the bright, still moonlight for quite some time after his tail lights had disappeared.

True to his word, he had kept their relationship on a 'no strings' basis but lately she had seen a faint light of speculation in his eyes once or twice when she had surprised him looking at her. As if he was testing something in his mind. The strength of his feeling for me? she asked herself. What my feelings are? Yes, I think so. And perhaps he's waiting for some sign from me . . . Would it be possible? I like him and I trust him, the kids like him and maybe we're two of a kind . . .

'What do I mean by that?' she murmured aloud and frowned. 'I . . . Yes, that's it. I once told him he was a loner at heart and I think that's true. And now, due to circumstance, I'm a loner. But maybe two loners, who respect certain reserves deep within each other, could build something worthwhile out of what they *can* share?

'Only I would have to be completely honest with him,' she whispered and shivered suddenly.

For several days the thought stayed in her mind. Then came the day when, from the moment she got up, she forced herself to think only of the most mundane things.

It wasn't so hard at first. The whole school was going on a trip to Toowomba to take part in an inter-school baseball competition. Matt had not yet achieved a place on the school team so Kate hadn't felt obliged to go, but she had organised a tuckshop lunch for the children and she was down at the school house by eight o'clock helping to load them, all their gear and their lunches, etc, on to the bus that had been hired.

'Now has everyone got their hats?' she heard Roy say to the excited throng. 'We don't leave unless everyone has a hat!'

'Sir, what happens if I get sick on the bus?' one voice piped up. 'I *always* get sick on the bus.'

'Don't I know it,' Marcie said to Kate out of the corner of her mouth. 'There's always at least one of them. Which is why *I* go laden down with plastic bags, lollies and face washers, not to mention spare hats and zinc cream for noses—you name it, I've got it! Sure you don't want to change your mind and come? Just think what you'll be missing!'

'I am. That's why I'm not coming,' Kate replied with a grin. 'But I'll be thinking of *you* .'

She waved the bus off and drove home and spent the morning doing all the chores that had been neglected earlier. Then she had lunch, changed her cool frock for a pair of denim shorts and a sleeveless buttercup blouse, tied her hair back with a yellow ribbon, and took the ute down to inspect her newly planted paddocks.

She knew she'd made a mistake almost as soon as she got there and she sat in the truck for a while, staring across the creek at her leased acres, waist high now in wheat that rippled and glinted in the sunlight and beneath the caress of an errant breeze.

She bit her lip and started the ute and found herself driving along the track to the old shearing shed.

It was cool and dim inside the shed and the only sound was the breeze whistling playfully high up through the holes in the roof.

She stared around and remembered how eerie she'd found it the last time. But today, the quietness and the shadows had a cathedral-like quality, and it seemed a fitting place to be in. She wandered over to the platform and leant against a post—and gave herself up to the haunting sadness of Grevil Robertson's wedding day.

She never knew what alerted her.

This time she heard no ghostly clink of metal, nothing. But she looked up suddenly with tears on her cheeks and the fine hairs on her body standing up in curious awareness, and he was there just inside the shed, watching her.

She gasped and blinked furiously, thinking it was an apparition—he couldn't be here, not Grevil.

But the apparition moved, started to walk towards her, and her lips parted and stayed parted. He was wearing a plain white shirt with short sleeves, and jeans; he was as tall as ever and his fair hair was windblown, and in no time at all he was close enough for her to see those glints of green and gold in his eyes, the faint freckles on his arms; he was no apparition.

She shut her mouth with a click then rushed into speech. 'What's happened? What's gone wrong? Why are you here?' she stammered, her grey eyes wide and totally perplexed.

He stopped right in front of her and stared down at her in silence for a moment. Then he touched her tear-streaked face with his fingers and said, 'Why am I here? For the same reason you are, Kate. I hope,' he added barely audibly.

'But I don't understand,' she whispered. 'I thought you were getting married today.'

'No.'

'N-no?' she repeated foolishly. 'Has it been postponed again? Is . . . is Jenny's father . . . Has he had another relapse?'

'No. He's out of hospital and fine now.'

'But . . . ' She swallowed painfully.

'I'm not marrying Jenny, Kate,' he said. 'Did you honestly think I could after . . . '

'*Yes,*' she broke in. 'You must. You *love* her. You're only feeling guilty about me. Oh, God, I thought I'd made you see . . . '

'You did. With the utmost clarity. Kate . . . '

'No.' Her lips trembled. 'No, I don't know what you're going to say but I could never live with the thought of coming between you two. I . . . ' She closed her eyes.

'Kate,' he said and her lashes flew up at once because the way he'd said it had been unusually stern. Their gazes locked and she saw grim determination in his eyes.

She shivered but opened her mouth to speak.

'No,' he said softly but with that grimness repeated in his voice. 'You did all the talking last time. It's my turn now. And you will just shut up and listen, my stubborn Kate. I love you, I love everything about you and always will, although I suspect there'll be times when nothing but a good fight will serve between us—such as now. So do your damnedest, Kate, but I must warn you I've missed you intolerably and intend to make up for it right away, like this.' He pulled her into his arms.

'You . . . you just can't *do* this,' she panted and tried to wrench herself free.

But he only smiled faintly. 'Can't I? Try me.' And his arms tightened as his lips claimed hers.

Some time later, they were sitting on the ground—at least Grevil was, leaning back against a wooden wall with Kate in his lap, his arms about her, her cheek on his shoulder, her hair coming adrift from her yellow ribbon and her breathing visibly erratic.

Once or twice she passed the tip of her tongue cautiously over her lips but she didn't try to speak and in her eyes there was the dazed look of a woman who has been thoroughly kissed into submission and not known it could happen to her. At least, not without leaving her feeling angry and insulted. But she felt the opposite , if anything—weak at the knees, clinging, essentially feminine and appallingly helpless.

She felt him sigh and didn't resist when he tilted her chin up with his fingers so that she had to look into his eyes at last.

'All right?' he murmured.

She could only stare up at him. He said, 'I shouldn't have done that, but sometimes . . . ' He grimaced.

'Sometimes I'm impossible?' She found her voice, but it was patchy; she tried to smile ruefully but ended up sniffing and blinking away sparkling tears and she turned her face into his shoulder despairingly.

'No,' he said into her hair. 'I meant, sometimes one gets carried away when one shouldn't. I had every intention of reasoning this all out with you— well, first of all doing that. But there's something rather explosive between us, my darling Kate, in case you hadn't noticed. Look at me, Kate,' he said softly but insistently.

When she did, he searched her tormented, tearful grey eyes and closed his own briefly. 'I know,' he said, smoothing some strands of hair behind her ear. 'I have to explain about Jenny. That's what should have come first, but will you listen now?'

She caught her breath then nodded.

'Jenny,' he said slowly, 'was related to Solange. They were cousins, not much alike to look at but quite alike in temperament. I've known her for a long time but after Solange died I didn't see much of her. Then about a year ago I took Tom to visit his mother's side of the family and she was staying with his grandparents. I . . . ' He paused and leant his head back against the wall but he was still absently smoothing her hair. 'I told you once how I'd gone about trying to find someone to take Solange's place. Well, when I saw Jenny again, she reminded me a lot of Solange. She had the same young, trusting kind of innocence. And she . . . ' He hesitated again but this time the silence grew.

'She fell in love with you?' Kate whispered.

He said quietly, 'She wasn't very good at hiding it, although she tried to, but she succeeded mostly in looking guilty and embarrassed. I found it very refreshing and touching. So, I asked her to marry me. But I promised her father—she's his only child—that I'd settle for a fairly long engagement because of the difference in our ages, because she was so young . . . ' He shrugged. 'I think Jenny was secretly relieved that she wasn't going to be rushed to the altar and then into bed. And then when her father took ill, it was natural that she should want to spend a lot of time with him. For my part,' he said sombrely, 'I was in no real hurry either. I told myself it was better for her to get used to it all slowly. Then I met you.'

Kate stirred in his arms and he looked down at her. 'And *I* fell in love with you,' she said, barely audibly. 'But . . . '

'Listen to me, Kate, before we go into anything else. It started to dawn on me quite some time ago to . . . well, to question my motivation towards Jenny. In fact, that day after the sports, when I was delivering such lofty advice to you, a . . . a sort of echo of my words stayed in my mind. I know now,' he said intently, 'that what I was trying to do was recreate what I'd had with Solange. That I thought I could take Jenny, so similar in some ways, and mould that innocence and trust into whatever I wanted. That I believed it was the only way it was ever going to work for me again. *That* was what I was going to do to Jenny. And that was what I told her, among other things, when I called it off.'

Kate flinched and sniffed. 'You shouldn't have. She loved you. What did she do?'

'She cried,' he said and Kate wept some tears, too. 'Then she was very brave and very sweet and she wished me all the luck in the world and we parted. Three weeks later, I saw her again, quite by chance. I was standing at a traffic light and she drove past in a small battered convertible with the hood down. She wasn't driving it but she was sitting very close to the driver, they were holding hands on the gear lever and when he had to stop for some pedestrians crossing the other way, he turned and kissed her on the cheek. She laughed and then looked around, but I didn't think she'd seen me.'

'She . . . had?' Kate queried, her eyes widening.

'Yes. And she came to call on me the next day. To explain, she said, although it was all a bit inexplicable to *her,* she told me. Because it didn't seem possible that she could have fallen out of love with me and straight into love with someone else, someone she barely knew.'

Kate drew a long, unsteady breath. 'Wh-what did you say?'

'I asked her about him. She told me he was only two years older than she was and studying engineering and that they hadn't done anything special so far but go to the beach and the movies. He didn't have much money and his car kept breaking down and he wasn't terribly good-looking but he had the nicest eyes, she thought. She stopped for a moment then and took a deep breath and told me that for quite a long time while we were engaged she'd been worried that she hadn't been living up to what I would expect from a wife,' he said ironically. 'And that it had made her nervous and tense but that, with him, she could just be herself and did I think that explained it?'

'Oh . . . ' Kate said softly.

'I know. In one sense,' he picked up Kate's hand and threaded his fingers through hers, 'I never loved her more or felt more guilty than when she said that, standing there looking so uncertain, so troubled, so young. I also felt about a hundred years old.'

'What did you do?'

'I told her that it was my dearest wish for her to be happy and comfortable and in love again. I think I convinced her to go ahead and savour it without looking back.'

The silence after his last words lingered. Kate looked down at his long, strong fingers twined through hers. 'So now there's only you and I, Kate,' he said. 'Do I have to explain that to you?'

'I . . . ' She frowned and bit her lip.

'I see that I do,' he said softly. 'All right, here goes, but it involves a confession which you might not like, so be prepared.'

She blinked and looked up at him, bewildered. 'My first intimation,' he said a little drily, 'of the curious effect you had on me, Kate, came again in the form of questioning my motivation. I met you and in the space of a very short time found myself alternately admiring you and feeling furiously exasperated with you, feeling concerned for you then wanting to take you down a peg or two. Then one day, during one of our innumerable conversations on the subject of how unhappily beholden you were to me, I caught myself thinking, yes, you are, Mrs Wiley, and if I have anything to do with it, I'm going to keep you in hock to me for ever.'

Kate gasped and his lips twisted into a faint smile. 'I told you you mightn't like it.'

'But you . . . you . . . '

'I know,' he said wryly, 'I denied it. Quite strongly on occasions.' His eyes searched hers and his expression sobered. 'Oh, Kate,' he said, 'don't you see? There was only one reason for me to feel like that . . . ' He broke off and grimaced. 'Well, I did try to tell myself it was because you kept flinging everything back at me and I kept reminding myself that I had, originally, wanted to help you because of Mike. But in my heart of hearts, I soon had to question that pure purpose. And I'd established an ulterior motive, although I'd refused to look it in the face before you ever told me you . . . '

'Oh, don't,' she whispered.

'Kate, I must,' he said gently. 'You have to understand once and for all. Something happened from the first moment we laid eyes on each other.'

'It couldn't have! I was such a . . . so . . . The way you looked at me said it all.'

'Nevertheless it did,' he said positively. 'There was a spark of something and it never died. Unfortunately, what happened for me was the classic way fools fall in love, particularly when this fool had convinced himself that it couldn't ever happen for him again and he'd decided to . . . simulate it. Not only decided but made all the plans, done all the calculations, tied up all the loose ends.'

'Grevil . . . '

'Except one. You,' he said. 'The loose end I couldn't tie up. So brave, so determined to go it alone, so unaware of the kind of hell I was going through until that fateful day I kissed you . . . so painfully honest . . . '

'I didn't mean what I said that day. I . . . '

'But you were right. It was an impossible situation and I guess that's why I got so angry. But then, when I found out the special kind of hell you were going through on May Watson's behalf, I could have shot myself.'

'I'm glad you didn't,' she said huskily and added, 'I looked upon that as my prerogative. I . . . ' She stopped and her eyes fell away from his because it was impossible to hide from him how she felt—as if what he had said so far was like an impossible dream come true, but she was so afraid it was only a dream.

'Then,' he said and moved his shoulders and settled them both more comfortably, 'I did something else I shouldn't have done. I took advantage of your distress that night and took you to bed. If I'd needed any more proof that I was deeply and irrevocably in love with you, Kate, that provided it, and . . . '

'But that was . . . that was . . . ' She looked up out of troubled eyes. 'I mean that was . . . '

'Sex?' he supplied.

'Well, yes. I mean, that's . . . '

'If you're going to say it's an unreliable guide, it wasn't in this case. Among other things it was the most marvellous thing that had ever happened to me.'

'You don't have to say that.'

'Shut up, Kate, it's true. And it wasn't only sex; it was us, matching each other perfectly, and it was *you,* everything about you that I never could walk away from, however hard I tried, and that's what made it so wonderful. Tell me it wasn't so for you.'

'I . . . I can't,' she whispered as a tide of pink entered her cheeks. 'But,' she took a breath, 'you said you shouldn't have done it.' She bit her lip and wondered why she was clutching at straws.

'No. Not while I was still engaged to Jenny. Because anything I said afterwards would only have sounded false. And that, my dear Kate, is the reason why I accepted your little sermon. But as it happens, I went back to Sydney the next day and put my affairs in order.'

'Oh,' she groaned. 'The wedding plans—your grandmother.'

'It was only going to be a small wedding and my grandmother took it surprisingly well. She said to me, admittedly after she'd got over the shock,' he grinned faintly, 'that it had often occurred to her you were a magnificent match for some man going begging.'

'Oh . . . '

'*Her* exact words, Kate, not mine,' he said with a glint of laughter in his hazel eyes. 'And having thought such, she said, she couldn't retract it now that man had turned out to be me. She also said to tell you that she would be very happy to have Matt and Serena and Tom while we go on our honeymoon.'

Kate sat up. 'They knew nothing about this! Does Tom?'

'He does now. He seemed to think it was a jolly good idea. Don't you think Matt and Serena will approve of me?'

'I . . . Grevil! You mean you told Tom before you told me?'

'Yes,' he said simply but with his eyes laughing at her.

'But anything could have happened!' she protested.

'Such as?' he queried lazily.

'Well for one thing I could have gone out and married someone else, well, got myself into a situation . . . '

'Are we talking hypothetically?' he asked.

'No! Jim Compton is . . . Well, I think he . . . '

'Kate,' he said ominously and with no more laughter in his eyes, 'are you seriously trying to tell me you would have married Jim Compton?'

'As it happens,' she said slowly and with dignity, 'he's a very nice man.'

'I know that. I've got nothing against *him,* but . . . ' He broke off, then said menacingly, 'You'd have found yourself unmarried from him pretty swiftly, Mrs Wiley. And don't ask me how, I'd have found a way, believe me. I don't quite know what more I could have said to you today, Kate. I accept that I've been pretty stupid, which might rankle with you, but I am not *ever* going to let you go so you'll just have to learn to live with it.'

Kate stared into his stormy hazel eyes and set mouth, and felt her heart beating heavily, and she thought, I must be mad, but this angry declaration . . . somehow I believe this.

She licked her lips. 'I only ever thought of Jim,' she said very quietly, 'because I just didn't know how I was going to cope with living so close to you, having to watch you and . . . I thought of selling up, anything.' Tears sparkled on her lashes and rolled down her cheeks as she remembered her agony and despair. 'I . . . '

His breath came in a sudden, fast jolt and he pulled her back against him and held her very close. 'Oh, Kate, don't. I'm sorry. Sorry for everything, even for not consulting you, for putting you through that. But the reason I took so long to come back,' he said unsteadily, 'well, there were two. I had Tom in Sydney for some medical tests that had been planned some time ago.'

'Tom? Is anything wrong with him?'

'No. But after Solange died it was decided that we should get him checked regularly—there's no evidence that her condition was hereditary, but just to be on the safe side. And, happily, he has an absolutely clean bill of health.'

'Oh, I'm so glad,' she whispered. 'Does he really not mind?'

'He said,' Grevil's lips quirked, 'you were actually more his idea of what a mum should be and he was thrilled at the thought of having Matt for a brother but mightn't it be a good idea to have a sister for Serena? Very wise of him and, oddly my appraisal of the situation, too.'

Kate shot him a grey glance and said softly, 'You don't honestly believe your omnipotence extends to providing sisters on request, surely?'

He looked down at her with his eyes full of laughter, but said gravely, 'Not sisters, no, but babies . . . well,' he shrugged, 'I'm sure Serena would like to have a baby in the family whatever the sex.'

'You're impossible, you know,' she said but with a trembling little smile.

'I'm also crazy—crazy about you, Kate,' he murmured. 'And that's the other reason I stayed away for a while. I wanted to get it *right*. I didn't want you to feel it was all quite so . . . off with the old, on with the new. I wanted to give you some breathing space. I'm sorry if I . . . Only I could have been such a fool,' he marvelled.

'No. No, I think you were right,' she wept. 'And if you'd come sooner, you mightn't have known what had happened to Jenny.'

'Then, will you marry me, Kate?'

'Yes. Yes . . .'

She moved in his arms some time later and took a little breath of pure happiness.

'I hope this kiss cancelled out the last one,' he said against her brow.

'All your kisses have the most powerful effect on me, Mr Robertson,' she replied. 'In case you hadn't noticed.'

'Ah,' he said, raising his head and looking meaningfully and lingeringly from her mouth, down her body to the long golden sweep of her legs and back again, 'I'll remember that.'

'What for?' she enquired innocently.

His lips quirked and his eyes teased her. 'For the times when you get all haughty and uppity, my darling Kate.'

'Oh.' She blushed and looked rueful.

But he smiled down at her and she smiled back. Then his eyes grew serious and his gaze dropped to her blouse. 'May I?' he said quietly.

'Of course,' she whispered and watched his fingers freeing the buttons and folding back the buttercup cotton and hesitating as he gazed down at the two creamy mounds of her breasts cupped in beige satin and lace, then drawing one finger lightly down between them to the clasp and freeing them.

She shivered in his arms and laid her head back over his arm and moaned with pleasure as he kissed them. She brought her hand up to slide it through his hair and press his head to her.

And later, when she heard him say, 'Here?' she answered, 'Yes, please . . . here . . . anywhere . . . '

He laughed softly but made a bed for her first with their clothes. And he made love to her beneath the broken roof in the dim shadows of the old wool shed, and she thought it was only fitting that this shed which had seen her sorrow should see her immeasurable joy.

'You know,' she said huskily—it could have been hours later, she wasn't sure, and she was lying with one leg drawn up, sliding her hand up and down his arm as he lay beside her, propped up on his elbow, the arm she was caressing over her body—'I love you.'

'I love you, Kate.' His voice was husky, too.

She sighed happily and thought she could lie there for ever in total, voluptuous abandonment and contentment, but she lifted her head and kissed his shoulder softly. 'Actually, I was going to say something else,' she teased, but her grey eyes were adoring.

'Oh?' He slid a hand into her rippling hair which had all come free of the ribbon.

'Mmm. All that trouble you went to to save my reputation and now this . . . It's going to create a sensation.'

He grinned.

'Grevil,' she looked up at him, suddenly serious, 'what about the children?'

He sobered. 'Kate, it won't happen. Don't worry about it.'

'How can you know it won't happen? After . . . '

'Because it's a little different being my wife to being a vulnerable widow, and before you take exception to that, my love,' he said with a wicked glint in his eye, 'I'm not boasting about it, merely mentioning a fact of life.'

'Well!' she said, but got no further.

'Besides,' he added firmly, 'my beloved grand-mama is another force to be reckoned with, and she'll be behind us all the way. However, on the subject of reputations in general, and *mine* in particular,' he looked around wryly, 'I think it might be an idea to get married as soon as possible. What do you think?'

She told him.

ATTRACTIVE, SPACE SAVING BOOK RACK

Display your most prized novels on this handsome and sturdy book rack. The hand-rubbed walnut finish will blend into your library decor with quiet elegance, providing a practical organizer for your favorite hard-or soft-covered books.

Only $9.95

Approximately 16" x 8" when assembled

Assembles in seconds!

To order, rush your name, address and zip code, along with a check or money order for $10.70* ($9.95 plus 75¢ postage and handling) payable to *Harlequin Reader Service*:

Harlequin Reader Service
Book Rack Offer
901 Fuhrmann Blvd.
P.O. Box 1396
Buffalo, NY 14269-1396

Offer not available in Canada.

*New York and Iowa residents add appropriate sales tax.

BKR-1A

Harlequin Intrigue
Adopts a New Cover Story!

We are proud to present to you
the new Harlequin Intrigue cover design.

Look for two exciting new stories each month, which mix a contemporary, sophisticated romance with the surprising twists and turns of a puzzler . . . romance with "something more."

INTNC-R

HARLEQUIN SIGNATURE EDITION

CAROLE MORTIMER

JUST ONE NIGHT

Hawk Sinclair—Texas millionaire and owner of the exclusive Sinclair hotels, determined to protect his son's inheritance. Leonie Spencer—desperate to protect her sister's happiness.

They were together for just one night.
The night their daughter was conceived.

Blackmail, kidnapping and attempted murder add suspense to passion in this exciting bestseller.

The success story of Carole Mortimer continues with *Just One Night*, a captivating romance from the author of the bestselling novels, *Gypsy* and *Merlyn's Magic*.

★

**Available in March
wherever paperbacks are sold.**

WTCH-1